UGLY MAN

ALSO BY DENNIS COOPER

Closer
Frisk
Wrong
Try
The Dream Police
Guide
Period
My Loose Thread
The Sluts
God, Jr.
The Weaklings

HARPER **PERENNIAL**

NEW YORK • LONDON • TORONTO • SYDNEY • NEW DELHI • AUCKLAND

UGLY MAN

STORIES

DENNIS COOPER

HARPER PERENNIAL

FIRST EDITION

Designed by Justin Dodd

Library of Congress Cataloging-in-Publication Data is available upon request.

ISBN 978-0-06-171544-0

09 10 11 12 13 OV/RRD 10 9 8 7 6 5 4 3 2 1

CONTENTS

ACKNOWLEDGMENTS

"Jerk" previously appeared in the book *Jerk* (Artspace Books, 1993).

"Ugly Man" and "The Boy on the Far Left" previously appeared in Scott Treleaven's art catalog *Some Boys Wander by Mistake* (Kavi Gupta Gallery, John Connelly Presents, and Marc Selwyn Fine Art, 2007) and in *Dennis Cooper: Writing at the Edge* (Sussex Academic Press, 2008).

"Graduate Seminar," "Santa Claus vs. Johnny Crawford," "The Worst (1960–1971)," and "Three Boys Who Thought

Experimental Fiction Was for Pussies" previously appeared in *Dennis Cooper: Writing at the Edge* (Sussex Academic Press, 2008).

"Knife/Tape/Rope" was originally the text of a performance art work of the same name created and directed by Ishmael Houston-Jones in 1985.

"One Night in 1979 . . ." previously appeared in the anthology *Thrills, Pills, Chills, and Heartache: Adventures in the First Person* (Alyson Press, 2004).

JERK

“Ladies and gentlemen, uh . . .” began David Brooks. He tapped his body mike to make sure it was working. Ping, ping. “The story you’re about to see is true, based on my own experiences as a drug-addicted, psychotic teen murderer in the early ’70s. But before I step behind the curtain over there . . .” He indicated a smallish, crudely built puppet theater in the heart of the auditorium’s vast, empty stage. “. . . and become the voices of my poor dead companions and victims . . .” He gave a little flick of his head, an old habit from the days when he had extremely long blond hair. ". . . I want to acknowledge . . ." He looked at the back of his hand, where he'd scribbled a note to himself. ". . . Professor William Griffith of the University of Texas, and his undergraduate class in . . ." squinted ". . . in 'Freudian Psychology Refracted Through Postmodern Example.' Whoa, that's a mouthful." He grinned. "Thanks to all of you for coming. Now each audience member should be holding a file. In it you will find two pieces of nonfiction penned by yours truly. In a moment I will ask you to read the first story. Later in the show I will ask you to read the second. They describe situations I feel incapable of representing adequately in my puppetry at this time. They also allow me time to move scenery around, prepare my marionettes, and so forth. So if you'll excuse me for a moment . . ." David grinned. ". . . I'll take my place in illusion." He walked behind the puppet theater itself. His half dozen assistants were already poised along the raised platform there, leaning over the stage's rear wall, string puppets dangling from their splayed hands. He caught their eyes, held up eight fingers, and cleared his throat, having carefully shielded his body mike. Then he took his seat before the music stand with its softly lit script. "Ladies and gentlemen," he read aloud, relishing the cool of his echo-y, magnified voice. "Please open your files and read the first piece of nonfiction. You have exactly eight minutes. Thank you."

Dean Corll, a dumpy-looking man in his thirties, is sprawled in an overstuffed armchair, thinking about his life, then formulating the best of those thoughts into a speech. About 5:30, 6:00 p.m., Wayne Henley and David Brooks, two thin teenagers, let themselves into Dean's house with a spare key.

"Boys," Dean announces, seeing them. "Sit, sit, sit."

The young duo flops down on the couch. "Hey, Dean," mumbles Wayne. David just sits there with his arm around Wayne's waist, sort of gawking at Dean like always.

"I have a . . . favor to ask you," says Dean. He rests his balding head back on the chair's filthy old doily and gives his living room a long, pained look.

"Yeah?" Wayne asks after a few seconds.

"It's about what we've done," Dean continues, voice a little scrunched by the bend in his neck. "And about what we haven't been able to do. What we'll never do, can't do."

"Is this about . . . what we've been *doing*?" Wayne asks cautiously. "I mean, the murder shit?"

"Yeah," Dean says, and looks squarely at both of their cute, jaded faces. "That. 'Cos I've been kidding myself . . . thinking us killing those boys was . . . like . . . an accomplishment? Only I realized today that there's tons of shit going on inside those boys' heads while we've been killing them that we don't know about. That . . . all this time I've been thinking, 'They're cute,' you know, period. So killing them was like . . . the big finish. But I realized today that we haven't . . . known them at all. Not any of them. So it's like they're not ours anymore, not even dead. They got away from us."

"Dean, listen," Wayne says anxiously. "Those guys are fucking dead. I was there, man. You're just—"

Knock, knock, knock.

"Who is it?" Dean yells.

"Buddy Longview," says a tense voice behind the front door.

Dean thinks back. "Oh, right!" He gives Wayne, David a wink and two enthusiastic thumbs up. "Come on in, it's open."

So in walks this boy, maybe nineteen, skinny, angelic face, kinda bored-looking, wearing a T-shirt and Bermuda shorts.

"Make room for our visitor," Dean says. Wayne and David slide to opposite ends of the couch. Buddy fills in the gap.

"Wayne, Buddy. David, Buddy."

The teens nod at each other.

"Hi Dean," says Buddy kind of sheepishly. He looks at Wayne and David like he wishes they weren't there, then lets his eyes go out of focus on one of the rug's myriad paisleys. "I've been thinking about what you said, man. About death and stuff. And . . . yeah, I'm sick of life. Definitely. I want to go. And I want to go like you said . . . make a big, fucking, gory mess."

Dean leers at Buddy, picturing what he eternally pictures—sex, torture, mutilation—but newly aware of how superficially he understands the young stranger. "Yeah, all right. I'll take you out, but first, as bizarre as this sounds, I want you to live here with me for a few days, a week, and let me get to know you."

Buddy shrugs. "No problem," he says softly, "but I'm a fucking waste. That's why I'm here, right? So don't expect much."

"Right." Dean reaches out for an old bamboo bong pipe. Even unlit, it stinks up the house like a big stick of incense.

They all get incredibly stoned.

"Time's up," announced David Brooks, noiselessly turning a page. The auditorium's lights started dimming. "It's four days later now. We begin the theatrical part of our story in the basement of Dean's house. Buddy's lying face down on a bed that's basically just a large piece of very thick plywood on four legs. Dean and Wayne have smashed the back of his head in with baseball bats. Once screaming pitifully, he's been silent for several minutes. Dean's fistfucking what's left of him. Wayne's watching that go on, mesmerized. As usual, I've been running around with Dean's Super 8 movie camera recording the murder for posterity."

Looking up from the script, David eyed an assistant who yanked a cord. Round front of the puppet theater, curtains noisily parted on four marionettes, like tiny human beings, posed against the first of several spare yet evocative hand-painted sets. As the Wayne puppet turned its head to "speak to" the Dean puppet, the real David Brooks licked his lips, preparing to throw the first of his finely tuned vocal impersonations into the thick of that fakeness.

WAYNE (*smirking*): So, Dean, does it feel like Buddy's dead? Is he . . . ours?

DEAN: Good question. (*He withdraws his fist from Buddy's butt, and stands there, arms folded, wondering.*) Ultimately, no.

WAYNE (*angry, waving his arms around*): Shit, Dean. You think too much about this stuff. Who cares what the fucker was really like? Killing's just about *power*, man. You can make up whoever you want and . . . like . . . imagine that person in this fucker's body.

DEAN: Really?

WAYNE: Duh.

DEAN: Like how?

WAYNE: *You* want *me* to tell *you*? *You're* the genius!

DEAN: Hmmm. (*He concentrates on the dead body, wondering who he'd most want to have killed today if he could've killed anyone in the world. Meanwhile Wayne and David go across the room and start French kissing. Eventually an idea comes to Dean.*)

DEAN (*pretending he's a corpse by flattening his voice*): Hi.

DEAN (*laughing at himself*): Who the fuck are you?

DEAN-AS-CORPSE: I'm . . . the actor who played the older of the two sons on the TV show *Flipper*.

DEAN (*mock-startled*): Really? *I* killed *you*?

DEAN-AS-CORPSE: Yeah.

DEAN: God, I had such a huge crush on you.

DEAN-AS-CORPSE: I had a crush on you too.

DEAN (*with a shit-eating grin*): Tell me that killing you was incredibly sexy.

DEAN-AS-CORPSE: Your killing me was incredibly sexy.

DEAN: Say my cock is God.

DEAN-AS-CORPSE: Your cock is God.

DEAN: This is unbelievable.

DEAN-AS-CORPSE: This is unbelievable.

DEAN (*laughing uproariously*): Wayne! David!

WAYNE (*unfastening his mouth from David's*): Yeah, Dean?

DEAN: Guess who I decided the corpse is?

WAYNE: Uh . . . Jimmy Page.

DEAN: No, no.

WAYNE: Wait, *I* know who. That kid you always moan about . . . what's-his-name . . . Luke Halpin. On *Flipper.*

DEAN: Exactly.

WAYNE: Well, it would be kind of amazing if that was Luke Halpin's corpse. I mean, the manhunt, the publicity . . . we'd be famous!

DEAN-AS-CORPSE (*stifling a smirk*): Hi, Wayne. It's me, Luke Halpin.

WAYNE: Hey, faggot. Good riddance.

DEAN-AS-CORPSE: Watch out or I'll haunt you.

DEAN (*laughing*): Cool, huh?

WAYNE: Yeah, Dean. Cool. Now if you don't mind . . . (*He goes back to French kissing David as the curtains close.*)

"And so," David Brooks read aloud, "days passed. We buried Buddy under the floor of a boat shed Dean owned. Maybe a dozen boys' bodies were already rotting down there. Dean killed a couple more boys on his own. Then one day Wayne told Dean about this drugged out, incredibly cute boy named Jamie from our high school, and Dean said, 'Sounds great.' So Wayne, with my help of course, cornered Jamie, hyping him about a 'party' at Dean's house, and he agreed to come with us that night. So, on the way to get Jamie, Wayne and I talked about stuff. I was unclear at that time about what Dean's TV character fantasies meant. Wayne explained to me how since those characters are only what you see onscreen they have no interior life at all, unlike real human beings, who are really complex and impossible to understand, no matter how hard you try. So when Dean imagined his victim was, like, Luke Halpin, he felt he knew exactly who he'd killed down to the tiniest detail, and that knowledge made the death more meaningful and complete. So that was interesting. And about that time we arrived at Jamie's house, sat him between us, and drove to Dean's. We sat around there getting stoned for a long time and eventually Jamie decided that being killed would be cool, so we trooped down into the basement, and Dean and Wayne tortured him to death. So now it's a couple of hours later. We're still in the basement. Jamie's lying carved up on the usual table. Dean looks down into the corpse's wide open blue eyes, conversing idly with some made-up person. I'm filming the scene, walking around, crouching, standing on my tiptoes to get unusual angles. Wayne's across the room covered with blood and sweat, experiencing some kind of existential crisis about having brought poor Jamie over here to die. I still don't know what his exact problem was, but I think it had something to do with Dean having taken away the only thing Jamie ever owned, which was his identity. Anyway, this is what happened next."

Dean (*whispering in the corpse's ear as the curtains part*): Did you like it when I cut off your balls?

DEAN-AS-CORPSE (*trying to imitate Jay North's chirpy little whine in* DENNIS THE MENACE): Yeah, Dean.

DEAN: You've been dreaming of this day all your life, right?

DEAN-AS-CORPSE: Right.

WAYNE: (*punching the air, furious*): Dean!

DEAN (*glancing up*): Yeah, Wayne, what?

WAYNE: Stop doing that to Jamie, asshole!

DEAN-AS-CORPSE: I'm not Jamie, I'm Jay North.

WAYNE (*livid, shaking*): No, he's not!

DEAN: Somehow I tend to take *his* word for it.

DEAN-AS-CORPSE: Thanks, Dean. I love you.

DEAN: I love you too, Jay.

WAYNE: You're *losing* it, man.

DEAN-AS-CORPSE: Dean, who's that loudmouth?

DEAN: Oh, just some creepy kid I should've killed years ago.

WAYNE (*looking around for a knife*): Dean, you *fuck.*

DAVID: Hey. Wayne, maintain. (*He lowers the camera down to his side.*)

DEAN-AS-CORPSE: You were into Wayne? Weird. I can't see it.

DEAN (*stroking the corpse's cheek*): Long ago, darling Jay.

WAYNE (*finds, grabs the knife he was looking for*): That's it! Later, Dean. Much, much later. (*He rams the blade into Dean's flabby back, pulls it out, stabs, stabs . . . Gurgling blood, Dean collapses onto the floor.*) Die, you fuck!

DEAN (*beginning his death rattle*): Glug, glug, glug . . .

WAYNE (*looking down on the corpse of his teenaged friend*): Jamie, shit, I'm sorry.

DAVID (*flattened against a wall, terrified*): W-w-wayne?

WAYNE (*still talking to Jamie*): I guess I just thought . . . you know, it'd be sexy like always . . . seeing Dean kill you, helping him. And it was, but I'm sorry, you know?

DAVID (*very tense and a little jealous*): W-w-wayne!

WAYNE: Jamie, I loved you, man. I could never tell you . . .

DAVID (*pounding on a wall behind him as the curtains close*): My world is *falling apart!*

"So," David Brooks read. "I just stood there waiting for Wayne to come to his senses. I'm a jealous person, always have been. Wayne's revelation that he loved Jamie was totally intense. I mean, I'd suspected as much, but . . . here was the news I'd dreaded. But Wayne kind of came out of his stupor after about fifteen minutes or so, and we wrapped the bodies of Jamie and Dean up in plastic, took them out to the car, and laid them in the trunk. Since I figured I'd heard the worst, I made the mistake of making Wayne tell me the whole Jamie story, and he not only revealed a ton of mini-orgies, but even more orgies with all kinds of boys at our high school. I was stunned, right? Wiped out. Some of these boys were supposedly good friends of mine, and there was Wayne telling me they were all smoking dope and fucking each other every time I wasn't around. We got to the boathouse, and buried the two bodies, and I thought, Well, at least it's over. No more killing. Hopefully, no more affairs on Wayne's part. He seemed contrite, just sitting there shotgun in my daddy's Cadillac watching the landscape zoom by, but . . . Well, I'm getting ahead of myself, ladies and gentlemen. House lights, please? Now, open your files again and read the second and last piece of nonfiction. You have exactly fifteen minutes. Thank you."

"I wish," Wayne says suddenly, then a fuzzy, subliminal, ongoing thought jells. "David, drop me off at Dean's, okay?"

David blinks at the road. "Why?"

"I don't know exactly," Wayne says. "I really don't."

The world's whizzing by the windows in two sandy ribbons. David grips the wheel. "Then I'll stay with you."

"You don't have to," Wayne says, not even sure he wants company at the moment.

"I *will.*" David glares at him. "But then we're *out* of that place, 'cos eventually the police are gonna look for all those boys, and knock on Dean's door . . ." His eyes glaze over with imagination. "Shit."

They drive on uneventfully. Darkness covers everything. After about a half hour David pulls the car into Dean's gravel driveway and puts it in park. Slam, slam. They walk around to the front of the house, up the porch steps. Wayne's feeling under the mat for the spare key when they hear a voice in the black to their left. "Hey," it says, "who are you guys?"

"Friends of Dean's," Wayne says, narrowing his eyes. Now he can see a vague, seated human shape. "Who're you?"

"Dean told me I could come by sometime if I was depressed," says the voice, definitely a boy's. "And I am, so . . . here I am."

"Dean's not around but you can come in with us."

"*Wayne*," David says angrily.

"Thanks, guys," mumbles the boy. Wayne feels around for the doorknob, lock, finds it, inserts the key, turns, pushes open the door, reaches in, turns on the living room light. Light filters out, hitting David and the boy who's in the process of standing up. He's a skinny blond with an unshaven face, sort of androgynous, early twenties, Janis Joplin T-shirt, holey jeans, altogether Dean's usual type. "Hi," he says, shielding his eyes. "I'm Brad."

"David," says David. He gestures at Wayne. "Wayne."

They troop inside, flopping on various couches and chairs. As usual, the place smells like a fucking bong pipe, and there's a permanent, almost invisible fog of hashish over everything.

"So how do you know Dean?" David asks, glancing meaningfully at Wayne.

Brad sort of chuckles. "If you mean where did I meet him, I kind of don't want to say until you tell me how *you* know Dean."

"I barely know him," lies David.

"And I'm more than a little familiar with him," sneers Wayne with what's as close as he can manage to a smile at the moment.

"Yeah?" Brad asks. He starts drumming his fingers on the arms of the chair. "How familiar is that?"

Wayne studies the boy until he's pretty sure from the look in Brad's eyes that he either shares their obsession with violence or thinks murder is a cool concept. "I know he tortures boys to death."

"Yeah, yeah," Brad mutters, still drumming. "I know about that too."

Wayne, David eyeball each other for a second.

"You want to hear something wild?" Brad grins at them. "'Cos, well, I'm fucked up. *Totally.*" He laughs. "It's hopeless. And it's just a matter of time before I kill myself, or let Dean do it. He wants to. *Bad*. Maybe he's even mentioned me to you. He's trying to talk me into letting him torture me to death. And I keep considering it. The only thing I'm wary about is the pain. Otherwise he can have me. But he's working on minimizing the pain. And I'm ready to die tonight if he's figured out a way so I won't be too uncomfortable."

"Are you gay?" asks Wayne, vaguely attracted to the guy.

"It doesn't matter." Brad folds his arms defensively. "Sex is stupid."

"Why do you want to die?" asks David.

"Well, why not, right?" Brad laughs. "That's one thing. Life is too confusing. And death just sounds like a great place. The worst that could happen is nothing . . . like, just becoming nothing, which sounds okay to me. But if certain people are right, it could be really *out there*. Demons and shit! Retribution on the living! I'm ready." He blinks. "So, what's your thing with Dean about?"

"I've watched him kill a few guys," Wayne says. "And I've helped out."

Brad nods seriously. "If you want to help him kill me, I don't care. Fine."

"Except Dean's dead. I killed him about three hours ago."

Brad practically jumps off the couch, awestruck. "You're the fucking *master*, man." He points at his T-shirt, on which Janis Joplin's tongue sticks out of her wide-open mouth like a bloody, bent sword. "I'm yours, if you want me."

"Jesus," David mutters, disgusted.

Now Brad looks carefully from David to Wayne and back. "You guys are gay boyfriends. I can always tell."

"Oh, *come on*," David whines, suspecting brainless homophobia.

"I'm not saying I mind gays. I'm just saying you are ones." Brad grins endearingly. "That's all. Anyway, Dean thought he was much, much more than just gay. Genius was closer to it. That's out of his own mouth, but I agree."

"Dean was smart." Wayne gives a little snort. "Definitely."

"So we can have sex while you're killing me," Brad says. "Dean showed me some home movies of him killing guys. I know how it works."

"Intense, isn't it?"

"Wayne!" David yells. It's a lecture compressed into a syllable.

"But it *is* intense," Wayne insists, glancing at his friend. "I'm not saying it's okay to kill people, but it was definitely intense to help Dean kill guys, especially the way he did it, because it was mixed with this . . . lust?"

"Let's watch one of the movies," Brad blurts, bouncing up and down excitedly. "It'll get me in the mood."

"I don't know where he hides them," Wayne says. "Do you?"

"Sure!" Brad jumps up and runs to this wooden cabinet next to the TV. He reaches behind it, brings out a key and opens a drawer near the bottom, dumping out dozens of film cans onto the rug. From where Wayne's sitting he sees the labels Dean attached to each can, names scrawled across them. *Robin, Eric, Colin, Buddy, Bert, Allen . . .*

"You're not *really* gonna watch one, are you?" asks David.

Wayne looks at him. "Maybe. Besides, you should see how they turned out, man, since *you* were the fucking *director* of some of them."

"Oh God." David cringes. "I should, I guess. You're right, I am kind of curious."

Meanwhile, Brad's been running around the room, bringing out the screen, setting up the projector, plugging it in, getting everything ready for a screening. Now he goes over to the film cans again, crouches down, and starts lining them up. Wayne goes over, joins Brad, studying the names. "So you've never seen any of the films that I costar in?"

"Nope."

"Which ones have you seen?" Wayne asks, starting to get a hard-on just being this close to the guy.

"Well, *Allen*, *Phil*, and . . . *Steven*." Brad points at that can. "Wicked film. Guy *loses* it. *Fuck*." He snakes a hand down to his crotch and starts squeezing. "Slaughtered." He looks dreamily at Wayne. "Oh, and *Bill* too. Excellent! And I think *Randy*, which wasn't as good, but . . . Let's see one you're in."

"This murder stuff turns you on?"

"Man," Brad whispers, obviously meaning yes plus an exclamation point or two.

"'Cos it turns me on royally." Wayne scans the labels. "How about *Wesley*? I'm particularly proud of how I acted with him."

"God, I don't know about this Wayne," mumbles David. He's still over on the couch, hugging himself really tightly.

"Relax." Wayne starts threading film through the projector. Brad sits cross-legged in the middle of the room. He straightens out his posture, hands on knees, staring straight ahead at the empty screen like it's the Maharishi or something. Wayne successfully threads film onto the take-up reel, walks over and flicks off the room lights. "Okay, here we go," he announces, pushing play.

The screen fills with red-striped leader, then it runs out and there's Dean's basement. A long-haired blond boy is lying on the usual table. Wayne's punching him in the face over and over. Dean's fucking him and trying to rip a nipple off his chest.

"Now see *that*," Brad says, rubbing his crotch. "I could get into sex with a guy if it was like . . . just the first part of my murder. I could kiss some guy and tell him I love him, and it'd be true, you know? Fuck, this is *hot*." He grins over his shoulder at Wayne, who's standing by the projector in case something screws up.

Wayne just looks back at Brad, wondering if he wants to kill him. "I understand," he says.

David's really hunched over now, wincing, watching the film out of the corner of his eye.

On-screen, Wayne is cutting off the boy's fingers with pliers. Dean has one fist in the boy's butt, the other hand around the boy's throat, and he's sucking the boy's limp cock like they're in love. The boy screams or at least his mouth is wide open.

Brad's longish hair starts flapping around so furiously that he's gotta be jerking off. Wayne's cock is hard too. David's just more and more balled up on the couch, looking like he wants to cry or something.

"Brad," Wayne says breathily.

"Y-yeah," the guy answers, his voice gone all wobbly.

"Maybe I *will* kill you."

David says something in a horrified voice but they're too concentrated on the film, etc. to hear.

"Excellent," says Brad. He peers over his shoulder. "But what about the pain?"

"Well," Wayne answers, "that's just part of it. You'll have to suffer a little. Big deal."

"Okay, okay." Brad turns back to the film. "Wait . . . wow, that's amazing." On-screen, Wayne and David are each sawing off one of the boy's legs. "Yeah, so pain's part of it, okay. I understand, no problem."

"*Stop* this," whispers David. He really sounds like he's going to cry, which would be a first.

"Why?" Wayne asks.

"Because . . . I don't know. Just *because*."

On-screen Dean has gotten what's left of the boy in a passionate embrace. Also, he's fucking his ass, which is a lot more accessible now without the legs. Wayne's standing by the table, attentive, laughing.

"Brad?" Wayne asks.

"Yeah." Brad's jeans are down in a blue infinity sign around his ankles.

"I'm a novice, okay? I've helped but I haven't gone solo yet. So . . ."

"Okay," Brad says hurriedly.

". . . so . . ." Wayne looks at the unwheeling film, sees the end is near. "I'm ready to start, I guess." He peers at the screen, which is pretty much dominated by splattering blood. It looks like a purplish-red halo over the back of Brad's bobbing head.

"Okay," Brad repeats.

"Time's up," David Brooks announced suddenly. The house lights dimmed to near-black. "So, it's an hour later now. We're all in Dean's basement. Brad's strapped down on the usual table. He quit thinking death was the ultimate experience about eight wounds ago. Blood's spurting out of numerous ditches in him, and several prominent details on his body are already missing. Wayne's standing over Brad, holding a knife, covered with blood, and smiling sexily, I have to admit. I'm across the room, bawling my eyes out. I'm also holding the Super 8 camera loosely in one hand, but I've never turned it on, not even for a second."

BRAD (*as the curtains part, using an unrecognizable baby voice*): Stop . . . stop . . . stop . . .

WAYNE: You don't mean it.

BRAD: I . . . *do* . . . (*gathering a little strength*) Life, l-i-i-i-ife!

WAYNE: You're delirious, man. (*He stabs him in the stomach and churns the blade around.*) There. That's better, right?

BRAD (*wincing horribly*): God . . . help . . . me . . .

WAYNE: *You're* a fucking disappointment. Jesus! (*He pulls the knife out of Brad's stomach and stabs him about fifty times in the chest.*) Oof, oof, oof . . .

BRAD (*beginning his death rattle*): Glug, glug . . .

WAYNE: Finally. (*glancing over his shoulder*) Cool, huh, David?

DAVID (*sobbing*): No, Wayne.

WAYNE: You're a disappointment too, David. This is *hot*. (*His eyes twinkle.*) Hey, who are you really, dead boy?

WAYNE-AS-CORPSE (*flat voice*): I'm . . . Jimmy Page.

WAYNE (*laughing*): I know you hear this all the time, but you were a genius. Fuck. *I* killed a *genius!*

WAYNE-AS-CORPSE: I agree. And thanks.

WAYNE (*still laughing*): And were totally good-looking.

WAYNE-AS-CORPSE: Thanks, man.

DAVID (*really sobbing now*): Wayne, if you don't stop this I'm going to have a nervous breakdown!

WAYNE-AS-CORPSE: Sounds like one of my fans.

WAYNE (*laughing again*): No way, Jimmy. David's into faggot shit like Joni Mitchell.

WAYNE-AS-CORPSE: God, I hate her.

WAYNE: Me too, man.

DAVID (*hysterical*): Fuck . . . you!

WAYNE (*reverting to his charming old self for a second*): No, listen, David. Dean was right! I'm telling you, this character projection shit is a real rush. Because I've decided this is Jimmy Page lying here, right? And it *is*. It's *him*. I'm *convinced*. I don't know how it works, but . . . Come over here, David, try it. Join me.

WAYNE-AS-CORPSE: Join us.

DAVID (*horrified*): Wayne, stop this, please!

WAYNE-AS-CORPSE: Loser.

DAVID: Wayne, stop it! (*Trying to get Wayne's attention, he hurls Dean's Super 8 camera, but it accidentally makes contact, knocking a deep hole in the side of Wayne's head. Blood spews out. Wayne collapses to the floor.*) Oh my God! (*David starts running around the basement looking for a telephone he remembers noticing once. Finding it, he lifts the receiver and dials 911.*) Hello? There's been a . . . murder. Twenty-three murders, to be exact. H-h-hurry! (*He breaks down crying as the curtain closes.*)

THE END

Three months later . . .

Dear David Brooks,

Perhaps you will recall that my class and I attended one of your puppet shows several months ago. As part of my final assignment, students were asked to write a short essay on one of the events we attended during the semester. As it happens, one student, Peter Winterson, chose your puppet show as his subject. I am forwarding his essay to you for your files. While I wouldn't say this was one of the finer essays I received—in fact I graded it a rather paltry D—perhaps it will be of some interest to you.

Sincerely.
Professor William Griffith
University of Texas
Austin, Texas

On David Brooks's Untitled Puppet Show

Peter Winterson

The puppeteer's thoughts are simplistic yet arduous, like a drunken walk home from a neighborhood bar. But his "drunkenness" only began once he entered the abstract realm of reflection, while the point of the thoughts themselves, hurtling madly about in his psyche, seems nothing more than the first word, or perhaps phrase, in an embattled sentence that has yet to formulate to his satisfaction. Between the murders he has committed and the artistry informing his puppetry lies a path so overly complicated by his obsessive need to reconstruct his participation that the actual meaning is subsumed by it, almost the way a libretto is dissolved in the music of an opera.

Thus the object of his artistry seems less a tamed thing than a vast galaxy whose organization refuses to answer to an existing law. Within its schematic, all ideas lose their consistency, all thoughts are corrupted, all feelings enter a state of levitation. The puppeteer's thinking is dislocated and each of its parts—images of images, derealized objects—displays an identity as defined as its existence is ghostlike. The feeling of mastery over things that intelligence gives him is great, but he nevertheless cannot possess those things.

This seemingly irreversible fragmentation of his ideas prevents him from grasping in their totality the very events which so energetically seem to solicit him, going so far as to touch the desires that are most difficult for him to admit. Forced to recognize successively all the qualities that compose these events, he cannot identify fully with them, or feel any comfort in his need for internal cohesion. He can only grasp the events by immediately dispersing them artistically.

Consequently, what he becomes aware of is not an emergence of things but a dissolution, such that memory appears to him to function less as a transfixed memorial to fleeting thoughts than as an exposure of the vagrancy of involuntary remembrance. Without privileged access to the moral codes through which his crimes acquire their meaning, his perception of them remains mediated by an encroaching emotion, compounded by his current sense of meaning, which is less about finding new things than seeing anew.

Perhaps these crimes would have disappeared into abstraction had the puppeteer not, at an irretrievable moment of sexual energy, attempted to understand them, and thereby awaken a childish response which refuses to yield to the formalist unity he now requires of his art. For while puppets have emerged, they merely confront his understanding with a hermeticism that is impossible to break open, further decentering and fragmenting his thoughts as they draw to them the emotion he believed he'd revoked, reanimating within their contagious parameters a set of desires he would prefer remain hidden.

UGLY MAN

Two months ago I found out I have a serious disease that's so rare it hasn't earned one of those nicknames like the flu. Even if I could pronounce its very long Latin name, the words would mean nothing. All you need to know is I'm being eaten alive by infections, and I'll be dead within three months if I'm lucky.

The worst side effect is a gradual, total destruction of my skin. It peels and flakes away in sheets. If I didn't spend half of my days in a tanning salon, I'd look like the moon. I'd have itched myself to death by now if my fingers weren't swollen into very painful, misshapen knobs.

When I was first diagnosed, my boyfriend said it didn't matter. But when there weren't enough porn DVDs in the world or a big enough increase in his allowance to give him an erection when we were in the same room, I cut him a final check and sent him on his way.

Now I buy prostitutes instead. It's obvious as soon as I undress they'll take no pleasure earning money from me. But they need the money just like I need to rub my husk against them. And I imagine they think that they've tasted worse and have been tasted by worse.

You don't know what it means to feel my chapped, disfigured lips and cock and hands saw away at something so downy. It's inexplicable. That's why it's hard for me to talk about the fact that my disease is so contagious a little peck on the cheek is enough to almost guarantee transmission.

In a few weeks, all the prostitutes I've hired will be the last boys on earth whom anyone would pay. Not long after I'm dead, they'll be dead. Some nights I fantasize about telling them what saints they are, but I don't. Still, there are times when I almost get the feeling they know.

THE BOY ON THE FAR LEFT

"Why? Because Prada offered the boy on the far right more money than I could earn in my lifetime to be the face of its fall ad campaign, and a portrait of him by Wolfgang Tillmans sold at Sotheby's for $350,000.

"Because the boy in the middle has dyed blond hair with an inch of mousey roots and wears far too much makeup on his almost pretty (from certain angles) face and earns a living having sex three times a week with some fat alcoholic in his sixties.

"Because the boy on the far right says he's only doing this because he has the hots for me, which blows my mind since he's an irrefutable god among twinks, even though I understand I'm not exactly uncute.

"Because the boy in the middle can't believe he's having sex with boys as cute as us and was only hired to do this porn because he's willing to let us double penetrate him bareback.

"Because the cameraman gave us the highest dosage of Viagra you can take without risking a massive heart attack, then we spent more than an hour doing lines of crystal meth and that combination is intense if you haven't tried it. I don't think I could stand up right now if I wanted to, and I don't even know who the fuck I am.

"Because the boy on the far right had one of his stories published in *The New Yorker*, which got him a six figure advance from Knopf for a first novel he hasn't even started writing yet.

"Because the boy in the middle got so stoned and drunk last night he couldn't walk, then suddenly burst into tears for no reason at all and told his friends he wishes he were dead.

"That's why."

GRADUATE SEMINAR

Artist: . . . and that's a work on paper entitled *Mirror Not Mirror* from my recent show at Hilton Perreault Gallery. Any questions?

Art student: I wonder if you would mind talking about your older work, especially *Railroad Tie* (1972)?

Artist: Do I mind? Yes. Do I know it's expected of me? Yes. Switch to slide tray number two, please.

Art student: I know you must be tired of talking about *Railroad Tie*, but, speaking as an aspiring artist, it changed my life, so—

Artist: Yes, I'm sure it did. Changed mine as well, as you are no doubt aware. Please show the first slide.

Artist: That's Ty Wilson, need I say, who, according to the history books, collaborated with me on *Railroad Tie*, and who is now of course very famous, more famous in fact than myself, even though he never made a single artwork on his own and did nothing with regards to *Railroad Tie* apart from appearing in it.

Art student: And being the coolest guy ever.

Artist: I'd love to argue that point, but a court order prevents me. So, for those of you who live under a rock, in *Railroad Tie* my work's celebrated (he said ironically) thematic interest in mapping the accidental (in quotes) was adapted to a mode of presentation that was soon to be, shall we say, au courant thanks to my pioneering efforts. Specifically, I photo-documented a teenaged boy's hitchhiking trip across the U.S. And there he is now hitchhiking. Next slide, please. And there he is getting picked up by the infamous trucker. Any questions so far?

Art student: Did you explain your art project to the trucker?

Artist: Naturally I explained the art project to the trucker, and, yes, he really did say, "So, if I understand your art project, I can kill this boy, and that would be okay because it's for art, right?" And, as I testified in court, I said, "The term art is being redefined as we speak, so it would be difficult for me to answer that question. Therefore, you must answer it yourself." Next slide.

Artist: I'm going to go through these quickly because you've all seen them a hundred thousand times. That's Ty being drugged. Ty lying unconscious in the back of the truck. Ty's reaction upon being relieved of his manhood . . . and of course, finally, there's the trucker killing Ty. Any questions?

Art student: What was it like being in prison for eight years?

Artist: What was it like? Well, my friends Andy and Jasper and Roy spent those eight years getting very rich and famous, and I spent them making dinnerware out of tin cans. And the millions that *Railroad Tie* earned on the art market went to a charity for victims of violent crime. And, of course, the late, illustrious genius Ty Wilson spawned a cottage industry of posters and documentaries and tribute songs and memorabilia that makes Jim Morrison seem like Bobby Rydell, a name you no doubt have never heard before in your lives, *which is my point.*

SANTA CLAUS VS. JOHNNY CRAWFORD

Johnny's psychiatrist gives him troubling news: Generous, gift-giving Santa Claus is in fact his sexually abusive father. Wracked with disbelief, Johnny runs outside and has a nervous breakdown. Supported by his psychiatrist, Johnny angrily confronts his lying, two-faced father. Johnny's father tells him to look on the bright side: Santa Claus has the hots for him. Standing outside his father's bedroom door, Johnny thinks, "Just because he's Santa Claus doesn't make sexual abuse okay. But on the other hand . . ."

THE HOSTAGE DRAMA

For this to make sense, you need to know a few things. Like that my twelve-year-old brother was gay.

`Click`. Probably would have grown up to be gay. `Click`.

I mean he probably would have grown up to be gay. He was even taller than me, and I'm fifteen. The doctors said Steven would have been around six feet five when he stopped growing, so he had a really long, weird body that was like looking at one of those bent up mirrors at a carnival.

`Click`. His hips. `Click`.

Right. He had hips kind of like a girl because he was growing so fast and parts of him were getting bigger at different speeds.

Click. You're making him sound like a freak. Say he looked like one of those skinny Russian girl fashion models but with no makeup and a cock. Click.

I'll just say that some guys thought he looked like a girl, and some of my friends were kind of obsessed with him even if they didn't admit it. And I guess he made gay guys go crazy.

Click. I'm a pedophile, not gay. Big difference. Click.

I mean pedophiles. He was like the pedophile's Marilyn Monroe or something. That's why I'm going to be killed.

Click. That's not why you're going to be killed. Never mind. Go on. Click.

I'm not going to be killed because I accidentally killed my brother who was your jack-off Jesus or whatever you called him?

Click. We've talked about this. You don't want to die. You'll lie to yourself to believe you don't deserve to die. It's understandable, etc., etc. Go on. Click.

What else . . . Oh, Steven had to go to this special school for weird kids because he had ADD and acted like such a fag. So all of his friends were weird kids like him who were either . . . going to grow up to be fags or crazy or both. For some reason, all of Steven's friends were younger than him, like ten years old or even eight years old. And now I should talk about Bree, shouldn't I?

Click. Just the basics. Click.

Steven's best friend was this eight-year-old boy named Bree. He was named that because his parents were hippies from France. They got shot to death right in front of Bree when he was six years old by this friend of their family because they came home and caught this guy raping Bree.

`Click.` It wasn't rape. `Click.`

Having anal sex with Bree. It wasn't rape because, according to my brother, Bree liked it, and they'd had anal sex a lot already. So the guy shot Bree's parents to death, and they ran off together and went into hiding. But after a while the guy got bored of fucking Bree . . .

`Click.` Which, having seen him, I find almost impossible to believe, but apparently there were reasons. `Click.`

Yeah, so he tried to kill Bree by poisoning him, and the guy thought he'd killed Bree, right?

`Click.` You're the one who told me. `Click.`

So he put Bree's not quite dead body in a trash can and disappeared. But some homeless guy found Bree, and the doctors saved his life. But he was always getting sick after that for the rest of his life, and he was just a strange kid in general. I mean, it was kind of sick how cute he was. Steven said little girls would practically have visions and Jesus sightings when they looked at him. And I swear to God I'm not gay . . .

`Click.` Except at gunpoint. That's a joke. `Click.`

. . . except when I'm tied up and being told I'll be killed if I don't do it, but I dare anyone who's even kind of vaguely gay to be in the same room with Bree when he's not talking and not feel gay.

`Click`. Past tense. `Click`.

Past tense.

`Click`. No, I mean because he's . . . Forget it. So talk more about Bree's problems. `Click`.

Right. So the only reason I can think of why Bree didn't get adopted by the richest people in the world or end up the boyfriend of the king of Saudi Arabia or something is because he was incredibly annoying. He was always really nervous, and he was always talking about how he was so nervous. It took about an hour for that to start getting on your nerves. At first people would be like, "Oh, don't be nervous, Bree. Everything's cool." But . . . I don't know if I should talk about this yet, but the other night Steven had Bree over to our house for the first time, and I was like, "Who the fuck is that?!" I started following him all over the house listening to his bullshit and thinking, "I'm not gay, but would it be gay if I sniffed his butt? I mean through his pants."

`Click`. Or not through his pants. `Click`.

Yeah, but I was crying with your gun pointed at my head when I did that. I think maybe I should talk about all the girlfriends I've had just to—

`Click`. Off topic. `Click`.

Anyway, shit . . . Oh yeah, Bree just kept talking and talking until the whole gay part of me went away, and I started yelling at him, "Shut up, shut up," and when he didn't, I guess I beat the crap out of him, and I guess it was so bad that he would've had to go to the hospital. So my brother Steven freaked out and started crying and saying he was going to call the police on me, so I freaked out and called my friend John here, who I thought was a cool, honest person back then, and who I didn't realize was just being nice to me because he wanted to fuck my brother . . .

`Click.` Worship the ground he walked on, actually. `Click.`

. . . and he told me to kill my brother and bring Bree over here.

`Click.` For the hundred millionth time, I didn't say kill Steven, I said bring Steven with you. `Click.`

You said kill Steven. I heard it. Why would I kill my own brother unless you told me to?

`Click.` Enjoy your last few minutes. `Click.`

So I got a knife out of the kitchen and stabbed Steven to death because I was ordered to do that, and then I stole my parents' car and came over here with Bree thinking John was going to help me. But he had a gun, and he raped me and Bree, and then he killed Bree, and . . .

`Click.` No, and then Bree died of his injuries from the beating you gave him. And you're just lucky you bear a very slight resemblance to Steven. Otherwise, it would have been, "I killed my brother, John." "Oh, really, Kenny?" Blammo. `Click.`

Whatever . . . and now John's holding me hostage and raping me all the time.

`Click.` And you killed your parents. `Click.`

What? Oh, I, yeah, I killed my parents, but they were asleep so that wasn't so bad. And now the police think I did it, and are looking for me.

`Click.` And you don't think you deserve being raped and killed. `Click.`

Yeah, and I don't think I deserve that.

`Click.` Which is where I assume your last words to the world should come in. `Click.`

Right.

THE BRAINIACS

It's raining, so a few of us are forced to get stoned. We're famously too intelligent to be a bunch of skateboarders, but that's all we are. Jules lights a joint, and we pass it around until the TV seems deep. We click through everything and compromise on violence. Then we realize it's just some political thing happening in Iraq, but we're too high by now to fight off our intelligence.

"Why don't we do things like that?" Thom asks.

“Do,” Jules says. He always seems the most stoned because he’s the smartest when he’s not.

“Blow ourselves up to kill people,” Thom says. “I don’t mean lowercase us. I mean uppercase us.”

“Because over here we call it suicide bombing,” Jules says. “Over there it’s probably called something that sounds really exciting.”

“Like what?” I ask.

“I don’t know,” Jules says. “We should ask that guy who’s from over there.”

“What guy?” I ask.

“The 7-Eleven guy,” Jules says. “He’s from over there somewhere.”

“You’re racist,” Thom says.

“You’re too stoned to parse out that word,” Jules says. “So I’ll let it pass.”

On our way to the 7-Eleven, we run into Debra and Barb. We’re wet, and they’re dry sitting in one of their cars. Debra’s beauty and serious lack of intelligence fucks with me, but I’m still stoned and can feel a kind of dumbness simulacrum going on.

“Give me head,” I say to her, and the guys go nuts laughing.

“Somebody’s stoned,” Debra says.

“Fuck, dude,” Thom says.

“When it rains, you guys are lost, aren’t you?” she says. “It’s kind of sad.”

“We’re organizing a terrorist cell,” Thom says to them. “You want to join?”

"You guys are spooky," Debra says.

"I'm serious," Thom says. "We're going to get some advice from that Arab guy at the 7-Eleven."

"You can be our bitches," I say. "Or we can be your whatever the opposite of bitches would be. Studs."

"Terrorists against what?" Barb asks. "Us?"

"What's that thing you're wearing?" Jules asks. He leans over and studies Barb's very cool sweatshirt.

"It's Denny Wear," she says.

"It's interesting," Jules says. "Where'd you get it?"

"On Melrose," she says.

"That's very, very cool," Jules says. "It conforms to your identity with this weird perfection that's kind of at odds with you."

"Let's go with them," Barb tells Debra. "What the fuck."

Debra looks from her to me. "You're serious," she says. "You're not just stoned."

"About what?" I say.

"About being terrorists, obviously," she says.

"Yeah," I say. "And about the other thing too. Just remember this because I won't. You know what I said you should do when I first got here? It's a legitimate and sincere request that has no expiration date. Even when I'm sober and distant again, the request stands. Don't be afraid to say, 'Let's do that thing you wanted to do when you were stoned.' I won't laugh at you or get sarcastic. I'll want it. I'll somehow unlock my intelligence and make it happen. This part of me is always there, it's just scared of rejection. Wow, I'm going on and on. I think this pot is laced with something. Thom?"

"What?" Thom says.

"I think this pot is laced with something," I say.

Thom shuts his eyes and studies his stonedness. "You're right," he says.

I look at Debra again. "Never mind," I say. "I'm untrustworthy. I want head now or never."

"Never," she says.

"You're being evil," I say, and hug myself. I feel incredibly laced with something wrong. "Just forget it."

We had to go sit for a while and let the scary lace inside us fade out. Since we're close to the stupid half-pipe that the city was forced to build for our skateboarding brethren and us, we end up sitting there watching these younger, less smart, better skateboarders trick around with their boards. I don't know about my friends, but the whole sham of us as skateboarders is so clear and crisp to me. After a while, I have to ask the younger guys for their opinion. They've seen us skate.

"Hey, any of you guys," I yell. They've taken a break and are sitting quietly along the pipe's edge thinking dumb, sporty thoughts.

"What," one of them yells back.

"We suck, right?" I yell. "I mean as skateboarders. Don't worry, we won't beat you up. We're too stoned."

"You seriously do, dude," the boy yells. His friends are just staring off vacantly like they're stoned, but I think they're just stupid and so their eyes are de-energized.

"Why?" I yell.

"In every way," he yells back.

"You're not being ironic, right?" I yell.

"Ironic," he yells in this voice I think is making fun of my voice, which I guess is full of my laughable intelligence.

"Okay, got it," I yell. "That hurt. Nice one."

KNIFE/TAPE/ROPE

Steve: So I was fat and weird looking since I was fucking born. So everyone hated me at school and everywhere else. I didn't care, or not enough to blow my brains out. So after about like third grade I didn't even want anything. Anyway, all the great bands are totally ugly too. Rob Halford, Bruce Dickinson . . . Ozzy. He's even fat, but that's not why I liked him. They're all just right about a lot of things if you really listen to them like I did. Thanks to them I made these friends finally. Ron, Jim, Jen. Nice people in a way. They had these criticisms of me, but

I accepted that. Ron knew all this stuff about Satan, which was amazing 'cos he, Satan, is pretty fucking ugly too, and even fat according to Ron. So I thought, you know, Teach me about death, Satan, I don't care. And it was all about murder, which was great because when you're not the one getting murdered, murder's the ultimate interesting thing. I totally agree with that.

Jim: I used to feel like there was someone else inside my head, but I couldn't understand what they were saying at first. Then last October Ron turned to me in psychology class and asked me if I ever thought about killing a person. I said, "Yeah," 'cos, you know, we talked about it a lot. And he said, "Well, let's kill Steve." I said okay because it was obvious Steve didn't mean much to anyone, not even us, and we hung out with him *all the time*. Ron said that Jen, who I think he was fucking, should come along too, which was okay with me. Then he said that he'd already planned that we should do it on Halloween night before even talking to me. He just knew I'd agree, which was cool, I guess. He's great. I mean, Halloween?! Steve kind of knew things were weird pretty soon, thanks to Jen. She's a really good artist. She draws these great medieval-type scenes that look like album covers. She did one of a giant warrior holding somebody up in the air who looked exactly like Steve but mutilated and stuff. And she showed it to Steve one day to see what he'd say, and he laughed, but he *knew*. I also think he'd overheard Ron and me maybe talking about it, I don't know. But I knew that he knew . . . just the look in his eyes like "I know you're going to kill me, but I'm not going to believe it." So Halloween day Ron asked Steve to come into the woods by the chemical plant with us. There's a pack of stray dogs around there, and we'd caught two and sacrificed them to Satan once, but we hadn't asked Steve along then 'cos he was too fucking ugly and weird. So after school, Ron gave us rides to his place. Jen was already there. We got high and played metal, and Ron got these baseball bats out of the basement. Then Steve knew for sure we were going to kill him. I mean, there were three bats and four of us. Ron threw one to me and one to Jen, and I could tell by his look that Steve was really wanting to have one. So Ron went and got a little axe from the garage and told Steve, "Here, you carry this bat, and I'll carry this axe." Steve really knew something final was going on. You know, four people and three bats. So we hiked to the well. We'd already agreed Ron would strike the first blow because he was the strongest and smartest of us, or we thought so. And it was his big idea, his bats. He chose Steve. And I mean, Steve was huge, over two hundred pounds and shorter even than Jen for fuck's sake. So . . . where was I? Oh, there's this well in the woods where we'd dropped the dead dogs that other time which was known as the Well of Hell. Some of us used to go there and pray to Satan when we were emotionally fucked up. The four of us stood by the well for a while sort of looking at each other, giggling. Steve was giggling too, which was really pathetic. There weren't any dogs, of course. Anyway, Ron chickened out. He just stood there staring weirdly at Steve, not talking, and we eventually went home. It was dark. Steve had to go home and eat dinner or something. We just watched him walk down the road waving bye at us feeling totally fucked. Then we went back to Ron's and put on metal and Jen drew this really great picture of Steve looking into the well, standing all by himself, with an evil smile looking at him from the water. It looked exactly like Steve. Jen said the smile was the smirk of triumph, which cracked us up. Even Ron. Then we rescheduled the murder for Sunday. And Ron said, "Let's make a pact that we stay sober this time," and that we'd get more out of killing that way. It's kind of weird to think now what was driving us on after failing at first, but I guess we just wanted that sort of experience, Jen and me from killing dogs, and Ron from dogs and from thinking about killing Steve all the time, I guess.

Jen: So Sunday Ron came over and helped my dad burn some dead leaves. And this kitten walked into the yard. When my dad wasn't looking, Ron picked up the thing and said, "Bait for Steve," and put it into a net bag. Jim came by later, and we drove over to his place. I think Ron was waiting for us. He looked cute. I always thought so. Then Ron called Steve and invited the jerk to come and help us kill something. The kitten, I guess. Then we listened to metal, and I drew their portraits 'til Steve arrived. When Steve got there we showed him the kitten and stuff, then we got in the car with the bats. Ron let Steve hold the kitten bag—I don't know why—but he started becoming too rough with the thing like a jerk. Petting it real hard, and that's not the way we ever did it with animals we killed, so Ron took it away and said Steve was a shit. We parked by the woods, and walked up to the Well of Hell. It takes about ten minutes. Ron had some rope, and we tied the kitten bag to a tree branch and hit it around with the bats. God, Steve was a jerk. He couldn't even hit it he was so fat. Then it died and we cut it down. I think I said I wished we had something bigger to kill. And Steve agreed, which was weird. Then Jim said, "So what're we going to do now, blah blah blah." Ron said, "*I* don't know." I think we were cracking up. Ron said we should smoke dope and think, but Jim hadn't brought one of his usual pipes, so Ron asked Steve if he had a pipe. When Steve reached into his pocket to check, Ron hit him right in the face. He started running away, but we chased him. He kept saying, "Why me, you guys? Why me?" And when we caught up to him, Ron said, "Because it's fun, Steve." The way he said it, it was real soothing like if you would talk to a little kid. "Because it's fun, Steve." I think that just freaked Steve out because he kinda stopped and turned around like, "Maybe they're not going to kill me after all." It's like he turned around on purpose, almost to see if we were really going to do it. Then we hit him like seventy times. Ron broke his bat. Then we said, "Sacrifice to Satan," and put Steve's body down in the well and went home. Like I said, I draw pictures, and I drew a picture that night of Steve down in the well that Ron wanted to frame. I have to admit it was great. I think it was Steve in the shape of two evil eyes under some water. I just thought it was neat, Steve as eyes, like he was going to haunt us. And I took it to school the next day, and I passed it around. People liked it a lot. They always liked what I did. They'd just trip on it.

Pete: Hey, you guys. I just want to tell you how cool what I think you did was. And there are other people who think so too, so you should know that.

Jim: Yeah, right. I heard.

Jen: You should really thank Ron, though. It's his thing, really.

Ron: (*mumbles*)

Pete: What, Ron?

Jim: I don't think Ron likes you.

Jen: Actually, I don't think he likes us, either. Or anybody, really.

Pete: What does he like to talk about? I mean, how can I get him to deign to speak to me?

Jim: Ask him about Satan.

Pete: Right. Ron, what's your take on Satan?

Ron: He's huge.

Jim: Do you mean popular or big physically?

Ron: Both.

Jen: Yeah, Ron told me once that Satan looks like Dom DeLuise if Dom DeLuise was scary looking. Or . . . did you ever see that guy who heads up the Satan Church in San Francisco, what's his name . . . Jim, what's his name?

Jim: *I* don't fucking know.

Ron: His name is . . . I forget.

Jim: Right.

Pete: Hey, great. It's hard for me to picture a scary looking Dom DeLuise, but I think I get the idea. And I don't know who that Satan Church person is, but I'm kind of more interested in what it . . . well, what it felt like to kill that guy.

Jen: What do you *think* it felt like?

Pete: I don't know. You're an artist. You understand stuff, not me.

Jim: I'll tell him. Nothing. That's what it felt like. You just do it. You start and then you just keep doing it because it's too late to do anything else. But as far as killing Steve in particular, nothing. It was better than killing dogs.

Ron: Definitely.

Jen: Tell the kid, Ron. Jesus. You're great and everything, but this kid's just interested. Tell him like you told us.

Ron: Okay. It's for Satan. That's all. And as for me, I just always had this obsession with killing things. I don't know really what it was. When I started out as a little kid, I couldn't just shoot a bird and watch it die. I had to tear it up. Same with Steve. I hated the guy, but I couldn't just wait and hope he got hit by a car or something. Besides, Satan sort of advised me to do it, in a way. He like told me, his voice. Jim, you know about this.

Jim: Yeah.

Pete: Cool. Voice?

Jim: Yeah, like he's inside your head with you. Look, you couldn't possibly understand, asshole.

Jen: I think he's cute.

Pete: Thanks.

Jen: No problem.

Ron: Killing someone is just one of those things that anybody who's honest with himself wants to do because it's one of the greatest things you could do. I mean stopping somebody else forever. Making them rot. How could you not want to do that? And Satan says it's cool to do it. Well, more than cool. I doubt he uses words like that.

Jim: He talks to me like that.

Jen: I see him as a warrior, a really big guy. We're like specks to him.

Pete: Cool.

Jim: Anyway . . .

Etheral Disembodied Voice: That's what you think.

Pete: What the fuck was that?

Jim: Did I ever tell you about the time we killed a puppy?

Pete: Not me.

Jen: I'll tell it. Let's see . . . yeah, we killed this little dog, poodle, inside a clothes dryer. Ron stuffed the dryer with weeds and sprinkled that with paint thinner and lit it on fire. The dog was running around inside, and it's the first time I ever heard a dog scream. It sounded just like a human screaming. We started laughing. We made it into a game, see how long we could make it live. Then we stabbed it a few times and chucked it into the weeds.

E.D.V: Cool.

Pete: *That*. What's *that*? Satan?

Jen: It sounds like fucking Steve, I hate to say.

E.D.V.: Correct. Being dead isn't any big deal, you guys.

Jim: I don't want to hear this.

Jen: Me either.

E.D.V.: It's black, extremely black. I can't even see you.

Pete: Do you like it?

E.D.V.: I don't not like it. Anyway, I just showed up to say that when you guys die, I won't be able to hurt you or your spirits or anything if you're worried about that. Death's weird. It's not about Satan or anything. You just die. It's weird.

THE GURO ARTISTS

"I do what you draw," said a voice. "But you can watch."

A tall, limp sixteen-or-something-year-old Japanese boy is tied in an X across a tilted wooden platform that seems to have been designed to hold a futon. His hair is many months beyond its last trim and dyed an artificial doll black, then combed out and way up and sprayed into place so it looks like a giant crow is sitting unsteadily on top of his head. His face has been paralyzed with injections of something, then given a boomerang grin thanks to a contraption the murderer invented and has hidden inside his mouth. His eyes are nonissues beneath contact lens imprinted with wowed, dilated "eyes" of a sentimental comic-book blue. Pinkish white makeup has been glossily applied to every inch of skin including fingertips and toe pads like the paint that killed the woman James Bond sort of loved in *Goldfinger*. He wears a little girl's pink T-shirt and very tight bikini bottoms made of black reflective plastic. Underneath them, his genitals have been subdivided into three lumps and neatly arranged there like chocolates. Apparently, I could hit them with a hammer and that wouldn't wake him up. Who was he?

"It's a strange question. Not much of anyone. He played soccer. That explains the legs and ass, as you will see. They doomed him. Other than that, he was noisy. He thought he was a clever child. His big head was indulged because his ass was so small and accidentally erotic. His parents believe he drowned in the river near their home and was washed out to sea. Now he is Flash. That's his new name. Flash is a superhero. His powers are great but he was unprepared for my lust. He didn't expect to be killed for that. He thinks Flash will survive like always. He's smug. He's secretly intrigued. But just before a bolt of lightning struck his head and turned him into Flash, the youngest superhero, he was a screaming, crying, vomiting sixteen-year-old boy whom I raped for three days straight, stopping only to nap and make some phone calls and eat. And before that, he was one of the millions of sixteen-year-old soccer-playing, iPod-wearing, charismatic Japanese American teenagers with an annoying donkey laugh, a cutely unkempt haircut, and an ass too exquisite to waste its whole life squeezing out shits."

THE ANAL-RETENTIVE LINE EDITOR

. . . I shoved my tongue deep inside his hot, tight ass [Editor's note: Many problems here. Unless your character is Gene Simmons, he'd be lucky to insert his tongue an eighth of an inch inside the ass, which, taking into account the volume of the cavity in question, doesn't qualify as deep. If he is a Gene Simmons type, you need to say so. Also, human asses aren't hot. Unless your character has spanked the ass in question vigorously—and there is no mention of that—or they are in a sauna—which they are not—the exterior would be lukewarm or tepid at best. If you're referring to the anal cavity itself, you'd be lucky to get away with warm. In fact, the tongue has a higher temperature than the anal membranes, so the effect would be a cooling. The only exception would be if the secondary character is ill and running a fever, in which case I don't believe the main character would be rimming him, correct?] and spent a delirious hour scrounging around in his delicious, silken depths [An hour, really? It's technically possible, but your main character's facial muscles would be very sore, in which case "delirious" becomes a problem. May I suggest "minute"? Your point would still be made. "Scrounging" is effective. It does feel as though one is being scrounged, but I would never have thought of that word. "Around" is unnecessary, but I found its masculine, blue-collar tone erotic, so I'll let it stand. As for "delicious," I understand what you're getting at. Your main character thinks the secondary character is very attractive. Hence, blah blah blah. However, an asshole is not delicious. There is barely any taste at all. It's the aroma of the asshole that creates the illusion of a flavor. Of course calling attention to that aroma would be risky. You might have noticed that most pornographic descriptions of oral-anal sex avoid the issue, apart from the occasional aside that an ass smells "clean." How ambitious are you? You could break new ground by eroticizing the aroma of an ass being rimmed, or you could avoid the area entirely. In any case, "delicious" won't fly. As for "silken," silk is dry and gauzy. Anal membranes are slick and greasy. How about "rubbery"? With "depths" we have the same problem I mentioned earlier: Your main character is not anywhere near the secondary character's depths. There is also the problem of repetition: "deep," "depths."] while he devoured [Is he a cannibal? If so, do you think he'd have the patience?] my big dick [Bland, de rigueur. Perhaps "gigantic," "monster," "humongous"? You could also indicate whether it is circumcised or not. Is the dick leaking seminal fluid? If so, that would add some pizzazz.] and juicy balls. [Oranges are juicy; testicles sweat and very modestly at that.] It took him a while, [an entire hour?] but that cute blond slut [I was going to argue against "slut" since you describe him as a virgin on pp. 13, 17, 18, 22, but, after conferring with one of my colleagues, I'll agree that slutty behavior is not a matter of expertise. Still, the word gave me pause, and it might be scrutinized by readers. Also, "cute blond" is too generic. I miss his "sleepy blue eyes," "small ski-lift nose," and "flowery pink lips." Could you remind us here? He and your readers deserve that much. I might mention here that I happen to be the "cute blond" type you are stereotyping in your story. Perhaps you'll think this throws my ability to be objective into question. Rather, I'd suggest it provides me greater insight into your story. Your "cute blond" could be far more human, individualistic, and erotic if you would be willing to go back and rewrite the beginning and middle of your story. I would be happy to provide you with more information regarding what your "cute blond" might be feeling, thinking, and wanting from your main character if you would like. We could meet for a coffee near the office during one of my breaks. How does Wednesday sound? This is not an editorial demand, of course, but rather a suggestion that you may accept or disregard as you wish.] managed to deep-throat all eleven inches of my hard, thick pole. [This wouldn't be an autobiographical story, would it? If so, what's your phone number? That's a little joke. Seriously, "hard, thick pole" is lazy. Sculpt it for us. Make us feel it in our throats. Also, isn't it the privilege of knowing his dick is inside the cute blond's face that forms the source of the main character's ecstasy and impending orgasm? Mention that. It doesn't have to be more than a phrase.] His hot, [too many "hots"] gagging throat [throats don't "gag," throats "constrict" or "convulse"] crammed with more meat than it could handle [nice] sent me over the edge, [of what?] and I exploded. [Cliché, cliché. Plus, it literally makes no sense unless your character is a suicide bomber. You can do much better.] Wave after wave of hot cum [There's "hot" again. Also, not to beat a dead horse, but sperm's temperature is not "hot" but rather lukewarm. Surely you've had enough sex to know that. "Wave" is a stretch—if only!—but I'll let it go.] gushed into his sweet teenaged guts. [Unless the secondary character has had a large amount of candy in his mouth recently, his guts would not be "sweet." If you mean sweet as in adorable, how do his esophagus and stomach qualify? Have you ever seen an X-ray? I realize you're complimenting him, but this is not the place. "Guts" is inaccurate, but I like it instinctually. It makes your main character sound tough and masculine. Lastly, I spoke to our legal department, and "teenaged" is a problem. They suggested "eighteen-year-old guts" as an alternative. Does that work for you? Frankly, reading the story, I assumed the "cute blond" was in his early twenties. Perhaps you mean he looks younger. I'm twenty-four, but I still get carded on those rare occasions when I go to a gay bar. It's possible I'm identifying with the character too much. If so, disregard. Finally, I'll end my edit with another quibble, albeit a rather large one. Why does your "cute blond" not have an orgasm? Do you find his pleasure unimportant? The ending feels very abrupt without it. If your main character thinks the "cute blond's guts" are "sweet," then what about his sperm? Are you saying your main character wouldn't want a face or mouthful of that sperm? Personally, given the personality you've chosen for him, I find that unbelievable. I can tell you that on the rare occasions when I have had sex, my partners not only wanted but demanded I have an orgasm in their mouths. In fact, it was only then that they were sufficiently satisfied to have an orgasm themselves. My experience is not everyone's, of course. I am merely suggesting that were your main character to take the "cute blond's" penis in his mouth and fellate him to orgasm, it could be the physical effect of this orgasm combined with the very potent, positive psychological effect of the main character's decision to take the "cute blond's" sperm into his mouth that would cause the "cute blond" to make the Herculean effort to deep throat the main character's rather large penis. Consequently, the taste of the "cute blond's" sperm combined with the honor of having his penis submerged in the "cute blond's" throat would give the main character a more meaningful orgasm and correct the problem of his callousness toward the "cute blond." It's your story, but I offer you my expertise on this particular topic in the spirit of teamwork. Let me know if you'd like to have that coffee. In any case, I need your rewrite in my mailbox first thing Friday morning. Best, Peter Guest]

Dear XRay Ted,

I've had an additional hour to think further about the edit, and I have one final suggestion. Let me preface it by telling you that I don't as a general rule give such a careful edit on the porno stories that are selected to appear in the magazine. I mean this close attention as a compliment. Yours is one of the rare stories we've received that aroused me personally in any significant way. This is due in part to the physical attributes I happen to share with your secondary character, as I've explained. In addition, the inordinate attention you pay to the secondary character's asshole and surrounding region happens to conform to my fantasy of what great sex would consist of with myself in the passive or receiving role. My use of the word "would" is a slight exaggeration, as I have participated in great sex or at least very good sex of the type your story emphasizes on two of the very few occasions in which I have found an objective reason to have sex. Thus, I believe I know what your story could become were you to take a little more time with it.

Pardon me for saying this, but your strength is not your writing but rather what appears to be your fetish and the passion your writing exhibits when your imagination comes in contact with a certain body part I'm certain that I need not mention. My strengths, on the other hand, are language, syntax, and other technical skills regarding the construction of fiction, as well as, to some degree, my imagination, at least when it is stimulated by what I suppose I would have to term my own personal fetish. (As a side note, I am currently studying for a master's degree in creative writing at Yale.) It occurs to me that our talents and fetishes are a good if not entirely perfect match. Hence, my earlier offer to form a more intimate than usual writer and editor relationship for the purpose of finessing your story. (As a second side note, I apologize for my long-windedness. I tend to become rather talkative when I am physically aroused. But I'll tell you a secret: There are ways to shut me up, and if I act hurt or indignant, one need only repeat the silencing procedure at length to make my mouth as quiet as a church.)

FYI, my limited success as a sex partner is due in large part to what I like to term nice-guy syndrome. Respect is crucial and a turn-on for me, but niceness is another thing. Truth is, I'm a nattering, self-absorbed tight ass at the best of times. I know this full well. Hence, when people are overly nice to me, all that tells me is that they're not paying sufficient attention. In my day-to-day life, people's inattentiveness to the unpleasant aspects of my personality is understandable. When fully clothed, I am not at my best. However, if I am naked and in bed with someone, and he makes too many allowances for the irritants in my behavior, and that allowance prevents him from taking full advantage of my body, then I can only conclude they find the gift of my availability unimportant, and, as far as I am concerned, the sex we have is doomed to be mediocre and listless, and I would just as soon go home and masturbate.

No doubt you are wondering why I have chosen to share this personal and revealing information with you. The truth is, during the hour or so since I last wrote to you, I queried my coworkers about you and discovered that I have been assigned the task of editing your story as a cruel joke on us both. In their minds, my obsessive attention to detail will "drive you crazy," in one coworker's words. They consider you to be a very primitive person whose behavior during your occasional visits to our office in the time prior to my coming to work here was sufficient grounds for any number of sexual harassment suits against you. If it helps, I am equally unpopular here both for the same personality quirks I have displayed in my e-mails to you, and because I happen to be several thousand times more attractive than any of my fellow employees. According to them, I was only hired because the managing editor of our magazine intends to find a way to fuck me.

In the course of this discovery, I was shown a series of suggestive digital photos of you that you sent to one of my appalled coworkers, and, deep breath, I would be interested in having sex with you with one proviso: that during our encounter we engage in oral-anal sex with myself as the passive recipient at great length. Actually, I am open to all ideas you have within reason that involve anal sex with myself in the passive role just so long as oral-anal sex is the centerpiece or chorus to whatever sexual activity my ass inspires

you to perform. My genitals are fair game as well, although I will forewarn you that they are merely pleasant looking and average sized with the one plus that they, like the rest of my body, are naturally almost hairless. My heritage is Scandinavian, if you haven't guessed, while you appear to be Spanish or Italian mixed with some Arabic, if I might hazard a guess. Whatever your background, you certainly do know a thing or two about large cocks. All the more reason for me to wonder why you slighted the one in your story. A simple pole, hardly. You could give that thing of yours a name and register it to vote. But I have flattered you and debased myself long enough. Shall we meet for that coffee I suggested tomorrow and, barring faux pas, take it back to your place?
Love, Peter

. . . The coffeehouse was swarming with trendy young pieces of college-age shit. Blondie was trendiest, but he was also *the shit.* [Ed. Note: I was wearing a Kenzo shirt, Paul Smith jacket. That's my current "uniform." Add?] The bitch must have killed when he was fourteen. [I did, but I didn't know it, unfortunately.] At twenty-four, he looked eroded—two flitty queen's eyes, a tight, disapproving mouth, and an already weak chin blurred by faint jowls. [This is painful to read but well written. Here let me say I was of course disappointed and confused by your nonappearance at our scheduled meeting. I appreciate that you appear to have imagined this meeting on behalf of your story, but a simple SMS declaring your sudden unavailability would have been nice. Perhaps you took my earlier discrediting of "nice-guy syndrome" into account and blew me off as a way of arousing my further interest. In doing so, you have misinterpreted my point. However, assuming this to be the case, my further interest is aroused nonetheless, which must say something unpleasant about me. While the mind-reading you presume in this vastly improved draft speaks of someone far more . . . shall we say, simple than myself (I will grant you determinedly less simple), I have decided nonetheless, based on what I can only interpret as the irrefutably heavy come-on you are addressing to me within the thin disguise of this draft, to invite you have a drink with me at Maximal's tonight. Shall we say 7:30? Oh, I forgot to mention that my "uniform" includes jeans by Energie, an Italian label. Include if you wish.] It took me all of three seconds to want to slam-fuck the priss until his screams woke up the president of China. [Point taken, but in China's political system, there is no president, per se. Perhaps you're saying your desire was such that you were rendered sloppy in your thinking? If so, you might rephrase the sentence thusly: ". . . slam-fuck the priss until his moans woke up whoever's running China at the moment." One other suggestion: Why not something on the order of ". . . rim the priss until his moans . . ." or even ". . . slam-rim . . ." or its equivalent? Granted, your main character wants to fuck the secondary character, and surely your main character will fulfill this desire (wink), but it might be nice as well as sexy to give the secondary character a modicum of respect at this point in your story. Not to mention that your main character does indeed want to rim the secondary character very,

very much, unless I'm misunderstanding your narrative, and I believe I am not. If I'm becoming too personal at this stage of our "relationship" as editor and writer, I believe I have the right considering my above-mentioned invitation.]

I like to know whom I screw. [Well, isn't that generous of your character.] But I'm talking know a little. [I saw that coming.] So when the kid started prattling [I do] about himself, [To be fair, when I prattle, I tend to cover the bases, and when I do address myself, it is only due to a vast insecurity. How about ". . . prattling on about things that were of no interest to me—things that were surely of little interest to him as well, a tactic of avoiding the topic of our obvious mutual attraction that inadvertently spoke of nothing but the lust that his insecurities and relative lack of experience caused him to try unsuccessfully to disavow." I suppose that's not very erotic. Rephrase in your own words?] I connected his dots—a face so fucking hairless, it must have seen fewer razor blades than Pluto has seen spaceships [Actually, I have about eight fine hairs on my chin that I need to shave perhaps once a week], forearms that made a twelve-year-old's look macho [I do go to the gym twice a week, and I believe it shows]—and it was all I could do not to rip his clothes off, lay him across our tipsy little table, and lick him off his skeleton like he was ice cream. [Off the record, my cock is so hard right now. I can be notoriously full of myself as a way of masking my deep feelings of inadequacy, as I said, but I'll nonetheless venture that your writing has improved dramatically in this new draft. Might I take some of the credit for functioning as your muse? I'm certain enough of this to risk sounding presumptuous.]

Call me big headed, [You? LOL] but if I want a piece of blond ass, it's mine. I don't even need to ask. [No comment] There isn't a man, woman, or child in West Hollywood who hasn't whipped their head around and cruised me on the street. [This is a decent explanation for your character's success rate, shall we say. Still, not to be the dreaded bossy bottom, but several of my coworkers here at the magazine have made the observation that you are indeed very hot while also giving you negative points for being, in their words, "too sleazy." In fact, one of these coworkers took me aside before our scheduled meeting yesterday to caution me against becoming "a notch in (your) belt." Clearly, I have proven to be a tad deaf in that regard. Nonetheless, should something transpire between us, I would hope to be more than a notch, or, at worst, a larger than usual notch.] Calling me a stud is like calling Mother Teresa a nice lady. Give me a Bible-toting, neo-Nazi virgin who doesn't even know what reaching puberty involves, and I'll give you back a walking, talking souvenir ashtray of the Grand Canyon. [Either this goes, or the virgin has to be eighteen, but it's interesting. That's your fifth reference to sex with underage boys in two pages. Working here at the magazine where every form of pornography imaginable has wound up on my desktop at one time or another, I've seen my share of so-called child porn. I'll venture a controversial opinion and say I've had to cross my legs at times when someone too young to be nude has stared me in the face. While I can't arrive in your bed via a time machine, I think I can say with some certainty that the illegal me would have blown your mind. I could bring along some old photos if you like? There's also fantasy role-play to consider. I will admit I've always wanted to try that.] So I let my eyes give Blondie some good, gentlemanly news while my knee drove it home with an ungentlemanly massage that pinned his knee against the wall.

"I talk too much," Blondie said suddenly, his knee struggling feebly to free itself from mine. [For the record, if it really were my knee, it would be returning the massage.]

"Why don't you take a little trip to the bathroom or somewhere so I can see your pretty ass," I said, giving him his freedom. [My question is: Would the blond character have done your character's bidding? I would say yes because he would indeed be hoping to "score" with you, and while I'm hardly the gay community's favorite cup of tea, no one's ever slipped a note into the complaint box of my "pretty" ass, as your protagonist just accurately phrased it, so, considering your main character's mixed review of "my" face and personality, a little show of strength would seem to be in order.]

"So we're entering the swimwear portion of the competition?" Blondie asked in his gayest voice yet, pushing the chair back and rising to his feet.

"More like the test drive," I said.

[Not to make myself completely transparent, but if, let's say, you had shown up at the coffeehouse as planned, and I'd ordered a drink or two instead of, oh, a latte—the vodka tonic is my nemesis, FYI—you literally could have had me on the table a la your idle fantasy of a paragraph or two back with that line. Remind me to tell you about certain tragedies that have resulted when the demon vodka tonic, myself, and a cocktail party full of gay men with nothing better to do have come in too close a proximity. In my darkest moments, I sometimes believe I have sought out a future as a writer, intellectual, and academic entirely to evade my true calling as the kind of fading, once pretty blond alcoholic you sometimes see taking on all comers in the blackest corners of establishments with names like the Cock Ring or the Eagle. Excuse this bout of unsexiness on my part, but something about you brings out the sad slut who whispers in my inner ear: "The only ivory tower you're suited for is waiting in some smoky room between two hairy muscular legs." Perhaps tonight, my love.]

If I'd been God, [as opposed to someone who thinks he is? ;-)] I would have slowed Blondie's fifteen-second walk to the bathroom door into a three-hour epic. His ass could have been shrink wrapped and sold in any sex shop in the world and not left a loaded wallet or dry urethra in the place. It was small and plump with two delicious fender-bender dents, soft enough to crown a sundae, as pert as the tip of a Norwegian kid's nose, packed so tight in designer jeans I would have awarded his ass-crack the Oscar for Best Supporting Actor on the spot. I could have sold those jeans on eBay to scratch-and-sniff collectors and never worked another day in my life. If asses could talk, he would have whispered, "Spread me on a piece of toast." I'm no scat queen, but I would have gobbled down his shit then licked his asshole so clean they could have turned it into an ER and used it to do brain surgery on my mom. While Blondie fixed his hair or took a leak or whatever queens do in bathrooms for what feels like forever, my imagination filled his pussy hole with the biggest load of cum in recorded history, filched it out, drooled it into his open, panting mouth, made him swish it around then feed me every teeming drop, blew it back up his hole, and fistfucked our soupy masterpiece so deep it dissolved into his bloodstream like an Alka-Seltzer.

[Speaking as your editor, this is perfect. Speaking as your hopeful date for this evening, and this might be stating the obvious, but, as far as I'm concerned, I'm happy if we hang around Maximal's just long enough to get a vodka tonic or two down my throat then high-speed cab it back to your place. I will add one forewarning: In the course of my exceedingly rare past relationships, one significant other wanted very much to fistfuck me. I was game, but, try as we both did, he was unsuccessful. My personal opinion is that our lack of success was due to his impatience rather than any physical deterrent on my part. But my asshole is rather tight at the moment due to prolonged lack of use, so patience might be the word should things between us progress to such a point. Also, should there be any question that the "scat" reference above is other than a metaphor, you should know that I would need to be very, very drunk.]

"You should have seen my ass before it was stuck at a computer ten hours a day, six days a week," Blondie said, taking his seat once again. [Something I actually might have said. Touché.]

"Bitch, your ass is so fucking sweet I'm gonna stab it with a drinking straw, throw you in a sling, and pretend I'm in my local malt shop," I said. [Idle thought here: Do you actually talk like this? If so, it's effective, I don't mind telling you.]

"So where do you stand on the issue of safe sex?" Blondie asked. It was a sneak attack I hadn't expected. [Those are awkward moments, aren't they? Real penis softeners. And yet it's an issue I personally believe more pornography should address directly, giving therein what I realize is a rather politically correct opinion. I'm complicated.]

"Not a chance," I said. "If a boy won't let me shoot in him, plunge my fingers in his sloppy, gaping hole, and rub my juice into his membranes like it was suntan lotion, I'm outta there. I get boys pregnant. That's who I am. But if it makes you feel better, I'd swallow a gallon of your cum with a sore throat and die shriveled up in a hospice five years from now with a Mona Lisa smile on my face."

[A bit confusing. I'm assuming your logic is as follows: Since the blond is a bottom and hence quite at-risk, drinking his sperm is more dangerous than were your main character to subject his ass to what I believe is termed "heavy cum edge play," because your main character is a statistically less likely to be infected total top. The question then becomes: Do you in fact intend as well as desire to swallow my cum at some point tonight, assuming my earlier invitation is accepted? I think that under the circumstances, that would relieve a potentially disruptive strain of AIDS paranoia that I seem to be struggling against regarding this unsafe business. Due to an impactful incident in my youth that I would be willing to elaborate upon when I am in closer proximity to your warm shoulder, I have come to equate the imbibing of sperm as a kind of stand-in for the words "I love you." Hence, such an act would truly float my boat. That goes for myself imbibing your sperm as well, particularly—I'm shivering—if it had been "filched" from my ass. Am I a narcissist therefore? Perhaps. Am I an excellent judge of a nice ass? It seems you main character would agree I am in theory. Being someone forced to have sex in a solitary manner more often than I might like, I have learned to simulate a certain objectivity about my own posterior, and thus I have come to the conclusion that its pleasures are numerous. Perhaps it would interest you were I to demonstrate some of my tricks.]

"Can I ask you for a few hours to reconcile this 'unsafe' issue in my head before I most likely say yes?" Blondie asked with a gutsiness that made me want to rape him with an AK-47 on top of everything else. [Goodness, that sounds so much like me I almost checked my desk for listening devices.]

"Take your chances," I said. "But you'd better hope my neighbor's son doesn't come home from school with one of his itches to use my PlayStation 3." [I like this in the story—although "school" is going to have to be "college." I certainly would not have liked it had you met me as planned at the coffeehouse yesterday and thrown it in my face. Anyway, I think you're lying. I don't think there is a neighbor's son. That's what I think.]

"Listen, I'm eight-five percent sure," Blondie said nervously. "Be nice. I don't sleep with people lightly. [There's the respect I was asking for in my last edit. Thank you.] These days, fucking is a life or death decision. [A bit didactic.] Picking you could be cherry-picking my style and date of death. But I'm ninety percent sure. Ninety-five percent even. Will you call me later?"

[Sadly, I can be the kind of tedious bore you're imagining. Still, let's leave that characterization in the story. Pornography needs more of what real tops and bottoms go through just to get a little nookie in the current climate. The truth is, were this a documentary, you could have told me you were so compromised by HIV that just lighting my cigarette—if I smoked, which I do not. Do you?—would be enough to "poz" me, and I would have thought if not outright said, "Please, sir, can you rip me a new one in the closest toilet stall?" Here's a piece of good advice about dealing with me from someone who's become quite an expert over the years. For all my intelligence and, to hear my professors at Yale, my promise as a literary talent, I'm slumming as a low-paid line editor at a gay pornographic magazine because I cannot seem to live for fifteen minutes without seeking suitable inspiration to achieve an erection. They call my condition a "mind-body disconnect," and, based on the research I've done, those thusly afflicted usually wind up in psychiatric hospitals before the age of thirty if they're fortunate. In other words, the voice you're reading now and will hopefully hear more than you want to hear tonight is to be taken with a grain of salt always. I am yours. Maybe you can give me your rewrite on a disk when I see you? In any case, I'll be at Maximal's, 7:30 tonight. I'm going with some of the boys from the office, a few of whom claim to have met you, so it shouldn't be too difficult to find me. I'll be the sitting duck. ;-)]

XRay,

First I must make an embarrassing admission in the form of

a quite awkward question: Did we meet last night? If so, I'll imagine you can understand the confusion with which I view the previous, oh, ten or so hours. Between the initial vodka tonic I ordered, at which point I recall scanning the patrons of Maximal's rather wildly for any sign of you, and the five (or last I checked, or rather could check) and presumably counting gift vodka tonics that my workmates seemed to find it so very amusing to hand and hand to the unquenchable me—a phase during which I will admit the identity of the person(s) under whom my greedy body longed to throw itself was sadly less important than general factors such as said persons' gender and the stiffness or lack thereof of what existed between whomsoever's legs—my night, which seemed to me to have lasted not much more than forty-five minutes, appears from the state of my surroundings and of myself to have in fact stretched until not so very long ago. Excuse me if this is rather predictable news, but I awoke perhaps an hour back to find myself unexpectedly seated at my desk in the office, or, more accurately, naked and arranged (by myself, it would seem, although I fear the handiwork of my coworkers is also somewhat in evidence) before my desk in a pose so melodramatic it deserved to be surrounded by students of a life drawing class. That, and the possibly irreparable shambles that was known until this morning as my workspace, and the taste of manly seed and, I fear, other less exalted fluids gone irretrievably southwards in my mouth, and the surprising discovery that my clothes appear to have been gathered together, rolled up like a small carpet, and used as a sex toy, then left half-protruding from my ass—something I could conceivably have done myself although it would be a first, let me tell you—clearly suggest the night did not conclude as my memory indicates with the happy sound of Prince's "Kiss" crosscutting the normally rote playlist that Maximal's employs and filtering down the club's narrow flight of basement stairs into what I believe was a kind of storage room while the objectively quite unattractive gym queens with whom I work every day chiseled my lower extremities into their personal totem pole like a pack of extremely ambitious beavers. That I appear to have brightened the night—if not the past, present, and future—of this magazine's managing editor, ad salesman, assistant designer, and at least two of the summer interns is rather humiliatingly not in question. The issue is who else may have come along for an amusement park ride on me, if anyone. If you were in fact here until not so long ago, I would appear to have enjoyed our first date immensely, and if the indiscriminate, uncontrolled me whom you could conceivably have taken great liberties with was so soused as to say otherwise, I'd like to correct that impression now. If, on the other hand, you were not in fact a participant in these undoubtedly raucous yet sadly erased activities, then let me assure you that, in spite of it having been close to a year since I last woke up to find this stinking, body-fluid-encrusted, pounding-headed, heavily tunneled-through Peter—or "Peter the peter eater" as one of my nicer tricks liked to refer to me—slumped in my usually dignified (in my own mind) place, it appears that I have lost neither the touch I've previously described to you at length in my meandering edits nor my vaunted gung ho spirit. For instance, I have such a nasty, splitting headache that they could stand me next to the Parliament building in London right now and nickname me Little Ben. Still, upon finding your final rewrite in my mailbox mere seconds ago, I opened it so quickly and grabbed my sore, exhausted crotch so automatically that, after a brief yelp of consequent agony, I cocked my throbbing head in wonder at the appearance of what I would gather to be . . . just say it, Peter . . . love, yes, love of a romantic nature from me to you. Of course I'd hoped to find an accompanying note from you of some lurid, grateful nature, but, needy me, I should have guessed you'd maintain the tougher-than-tough-guy stance that has so riveted my thoughts of you thus far. Still, if you were indeed there last night, I must wonder why I have not received a pleasant SMS. On second thought, scratch that, as I appear to have misplaced my cell phone at some point during last night's festivities, unless it happened to join my clothing in the septic tank formerly known as my quote-unquote "steaming hot boy pussy," though I suppose I would know were that the case. If my supposing is incorrect, let's hope it's set to vibrate mode. A terrible quip, I know. Before I try to tidy up and head home for a shower that should singlehandedly get the "no swimming" signs set up on Santa Monica Beach, I'll use this strangely golden opportunity to lend what remains of my editing expertise to what I might boldly call our little collaborative XXX-rated masterpiece. Note that normally I would have read your draft up to eight times with great care and filled a second, corresponding Word document with copious notes before offering my suggestions, but, given the circumstances I've described plus the demands of an entirely sincere if beleaguered erection given me by the mere appearance of your name in my e-mail in-box, I think it best to preserve my waning energies and tackle the text at hand cold. So, let me see . . .

OLIVER TWINK

Chris?

What?

Chris.

What.

How long have you lived here?

I don't know.

It's been exactly three and a half months tonight.

Yeah, I guess.

A lot's changed.

I guess. What do you mean?

Well, for one thing, you were only shooting dope once a day then.

About, yeah.

Sometimes twice.

Yeah. Something like that.

I mean you weren't a full-blown junkie like

you are now.
Sorry.

No, you're right.
That was stupid.

What was?

I should've never
started doing this
much.

Because how
much do you do
now?

A day?

Yeah.

Fuck. Three shots,
I guess.

Actually, it's five.

No it isn't. Oh
wait, yeah,
sometimes.

Thanks to me.

What?

I just mean I'm
paying for it.

Fuck, you're going
to pull that shit?

That's not what
I'm saying.

Fuck you. You're
the one that wanted
to be my fucking
uncle.

I never said that.
That's your take.

I hate it when you
pull this shit.

Calm down.

Shut up. God.

You're ruining your high.

You're ruining it, you fuck. Jesus.

Calm down. I was just saying . . .

What.

That we've known each other for a while now. That we've been through a lot.

Yeah.

That's all.

Okay.

And it's been great to know you.

Yeah, well, that cuts both ways.

What do you mean?

I don't want to get into it.

Go ahead.

Look, you help me out. You give me all this shit, but I'm fucked, aren't I? I mean what the fuck do I do?

You do what you want.

I don't know. Maybe you shouldn't just give me shit. Maybe if you told me to fuck off, I'd stop doing dope and . . . Fuck, I don't know.

Get a job?

Who knows? That's the fucking point.

But it's too late.

What?

It's too late. This is what you are. It's what you wanted. You said so. You wanted it to be easy.

Yeah, when I was fucking . . . I'm only fucking nineteen.

What would you do?

I don't know.

Look, you've got problems, deep problems.

Oh, great.

You went on anti-depressants when you were . . . what, seven? You did nothing but get into trouble. You had no close friends, no money. You never wanted to do anything. You don't speak to your parents. You don't have a single friend left. Right?

Yeah, yeah.

Your whole life

you've either been suicidal or you've blown up and alienated everyone.

Shit.

What?

Nothing. I'm just agreeing with you.

But I understand you. You hate it, but I'm the only person who's stuck it out with you.

Whatever.

And I haven't asked you for anything.

Yeah, but you ask for a lot.

Your company.

You practically own me, you know? It's fucked up.

I don't own you.

Yeah, you fucking do. You and getting loaded are my whole fucking world now. You could throw me out, and I'd be fucked.

But you know I wouldn't.

No, I don't know that. It's fucked up. You're all generous and obsessed or whatever with me and shit, but you have all the power. It's like a fucking game.

That's the heroin talking.

Yeah, but what have you gotten out of it? And don't say I'm such a great guy, and it's just great to be around me.

It's true. Well, I don't know about great. Interesting for sure.

Come on. I'm a fucking . . . I watch TV. I listen to music you hate.

You're surprisingly interesting—

Interesting?

To me, you are.

Jesus, I treat you
like shit.

I know you really well, okay? In some ways, much better than you know yourself.

This is what I
mean.

What?

I don't know. That
it's confusing.
Fuck.

What's confusing?

What do you mean
"what's
confusing"?

I mean what are you thinking?

Nothing.

Say it.

Say what?

What you're thinking.

What I'm thinking? I'm thinking I wish I was dead. I'm thinking what I always think. Who fucking cares? It's boring.

That's interesting.

I'm sure it is to you.

Okay.

What, that's not
interesting to you?

Obviously, it is.

Okay, then.

So . . . ?

So . . . Fuck.

What?

Okay, I'm thinking
maybe I should do
something for you.
I never do shit for
you.

Like what?

What could I do
for you that would
be really great?

**What do you have
in mind?**

I don't know.

Do you want me to think of something?

Yeah, if you want to. I don't know. The only thing I can think of . . . but I don't know if you still want it . . .

What?

You remember that time . . . Shit, that time we had that talk about . . . you know?

We've had a lot of talks.

You know what I mean. When I was here that first night. I thought you were . . . you know, that you were being nice to me because . . . Fuck, you know what I'm talking about.

Because I wanted to fuck you.

Yeah, but you said . . . shit, you know what you said.

What did I say?

Fuck you.

What?

You fucking remember what you said. I'm not going to say it.

I remember.

Okay, so you said that it wasn't just about you fucking me because you were into that other thing, but that, yeah, you thought I was good looking.

I think what I said was that I would fuck you in a millisecond.

Yeah. Well, I guess you sort of got over that.

No, I didn't.

Yeah, right.

I still think you'd be an amazing fuck.

Right.

I do.

What, are you fucking nuts? I'm sorry.

There's just something about you. It's not just the looks, although there's this tragedy to you, to what the drugs have done to your looks, that's incredibly hot. You've gone from really cute to beautiful in this scary, profound way. But it's not physical. It's the whole thing. It's the way you are, the way you move, the fucked-up shit, the boring stuff, what

a loser you are,
the whole thing.
It just gets to me.
You turn me on
even more than
you used to, since
you asked.

Yeah, right.

You'll be nodding
out, watching TV,
whatever, and I'll
get hard just
looking at you.
Sometimes when
you're out of it, I
bury my face in
your crotch just
to smell you.

Yeah, well, I know
that.

Yeah, just
to know what
having you would
be like.

Okay, that's
enough of that.

That's just one example. You don't even want to know.

Shit. If you'd said that a month ago, I would've fucking . . .

What?

I don't know.
That's fucked up.

You would have had sex with me, or . . . ?

No. I don't know.
I don't even remember . . .

Remember . . .

I don't know. You know, why? Why, you know . . . I don't know. Fuck, I hate myself.

I know.

I'm so fucked up. I'm just a waste. I just drain the fucking world. I'm just a fucking pain in the ass. There's just nothing about me that means any fucking thing. I hate that I'm fucking alive.

I understand.

I know you fucking do.

Go ahead and cry. I don't mind.

Fuck. I'm so
fucking selfish,
and I don't even
know what I want.
I don't understand
myself. I never
did. I don't know
why I do things or
don't do things,
and then I don't
fucking do
anything, and I'm
such a fucking
asshole. I really
fucking hate
myself.

**You shouldn't,
but you've never
let anyone help
you.**

I let you help me.

**Yeah, in your
own weird way.**

I want you to help

me, okay? It's just . . . I never understood why. I don't understand anything. I'm afraid of you. I'm afraid of my fucking self, you know?

I know.

You know, a month ago . . . It's just, I don't know.

What?

I thought about it.

About what?

You know. Just sort of . . . you know. Fuck, you know what I mean.

Sleeping with me.

Yeah, but . . . Fuck. Why are you doing this shit? You know what I mean.

I want you to say it.

Why?

Because I need to know you really want it. I need to know that you're sure.

I'm sure.

Then say it. Make it real.

Fuck. I want . . . I'm just going to say it like this, because . . . I hate that you're making me do this. Don't fucking look at me.

I thought about
what if . . . I wanted
to be with God?
Would that be like
your big dream
come true?

Honestly?

Yeah.

**If you mean if you
were dead, yeah.
If it were you,
yeah.**

It makes a
difference that it's
me.

A huge difference.

Why?

**Because I'd know
who was dying so
it would be heavy
and tragic. You'd**

be here, and then you wouldn't. You'd just be something that looks like you. And then it would look less and less like you until you were just a corpse, a male corpse.

Because I'd rot.

I wouldn't let you rot. I'd fuck you for a while and then burn you or dismember you or bury you.

Wait. After I was dead?

I honestly don't know.

You haven't said anything about that

in a while.

Really?

Yeah, you used to say things. You used to make these weird jokes about it.

I think it's too real to be funny now.

So you're not going to kill me?

I was, but . . . I don't know. I haven't done it, have I? So I honestly don't know. I think I waited too long. Maybe I never really wanted to anyway. Maybe it was just an idea.

So you aren't
going to?

**Why, do you want
me to?**

No. I don't know.
When I think about
killing myself
sometimes, I do.
But maybe that's
because I can't do
it myself. All I
have to do is shoot
too much dope, but
I just can't. I've
tried a couple of
times, obviously.

I know.

But you didn't let
me die.

**I didn't want it to
happen like that.**

I could have made myself

OD when you weren't
around, but I guess
I was afraid to.

Yeah, well, please
don't.

I won't. Wow,
that's kind of cool.

What is?

You saying please
don't.

You know . . .
honestly, you're
very sweet. It's a
shame. You
really had
possibilities.

That's cool.

But I meant
please don't
because I don't
want to have to

deal with it. I'd have to . . . deal with it, you know? I mean with your body and the guilt and all of that.

Oh, right. That would be fucked up.

But . . . I also don't want you to die because I just don't want you to, okay?

Okay.

I can't believe I told you that.

So you don't want to be boyfriends?

I don't think you

even know what that means.

I know what boyfriends means. I'm not a fucking idiot. I had gay friends and shit. I just think that way I could do something useful, and maybe you'd give me some money, and you'd maybe get off on that.

That's what you meant?

Yeah, what did you think?

I thought you meant boyfriends. Like normal in love boyfriends.

Yeah, well . . . yeah, I did. I just thought that's how you wanted it.

But aren't you straight? I mean you've always made this big deal about how you're straight.

Fuck off.

And . . . look, I'm sort of . . . I'm not sure if I . . .

It's okay. Forget it.

No, listen. The boyfriend thing . . . I've never even considered it.

Forget it.

No, I'm saying maybe that's the answer. I'm just not sure.

I don't care.

Yeah, you do.

No, why would I? Oh, you mean you're going to throw me out?

What?

You're going to kick me out.

Where the hell did that come from?

You will. I fucking know it. I never should have said that. God, I hate you.

No, that's the problem. I don't want to throw you out. I know how horrible that would be for you. I've put you and me in this total mess. There's no solution, and I don't know what in the hell to do.

Yeah, you do. You want me dead so you can do your sex thing and then feel sad that I'm dead or whatever. You just said that.

Ideally, yeah. Realistically, no.

Didn't you say that?

Basically.

Then I don't understand.

It's not a realistic idea.

But I've fucked everything up, and you never made it seem like I was so . . . Oh, forget it. Whatever. I really don't care.

Look, you're straight.

Fuck you.

And you're a junkie. You chose that. You don't care about anything but doing dope.

How do you fucking know?

What, I'm wrong?

I . . . Fuck, man.

What?

You know what I'm going to say.

No, I don't. This is your problem. You don't give me anything. You just assume I'm so interested in you that I know what you think.

Fuck. You don't love me.

What?

You don't love me, right? You don't fucking love me, right? That's what you're saying.

You're not even gay. You're such a junkie, you don't even think about things like that.

Fuck off.

What?

You know fucking what. Shit.

I honestly don't.

Fuck you. You know I'm gay. You know I just can't fucking deal with it. I hate that you do that. I just hate that you do that.

Chris.

What?!

I don't think you know what you are.

Yeah, I do.

Then why haven't you given me a sign? I would have fucked you in a second. You know that. You knew it would have been a disaster, but I would have done it in a second.

You know why I didn't.

Because you aren't really gay and when you thought about the sex you couldn't do it.

No, because people want what they can't have and all that shit. They make things they can't have into more than they are, and . . . you know, that's the one thing I had, that I have, that you . . . like me or whatever so much and it doesn't make any sense.

It makes total sense.

Yeah, well, I don't think so.

Look, from your perspective, have you ever had anyone in your life like me, who accepts you so

unconditionally,
who wants to
spend all their
time with you,
and who gives you
anything you
want?

Yeah, my uncle.

Who you loved.

Yeah, and who
fucking died
because of me.

So what else do
you need to
know?

What? I don't
know what the
fuck you're saying.

Your paranoia
aside, I've never
wavered in my
interest in you.

What are you saying?

I don't know what I'm saying. I'm just saying it.

Forget it. It's just fucking bullshit anyway.

What is?

You want to fuck me but you don't want to fuck me or I don't know.

I do.

Bullshit. I don't want to do it anyway. You'd just hate me after that.

You're the one who'd hate me.

No, I wouldn't.

Why, what do you think you'd feel?

It depends on what you felt.

What do you think I'd feel?

That I'm an ugly, skinny piece of shit who's boring in bed.

You don't get it.

What?

Do you think you're that hot? Has your life been filled with guys and girls obsessing on sleeping with you? Waiting and waiting and

doing anything they had to do to fuck you, no matter how long it took?

No, no. Fucking hardly.

Okay.

Yeah, okay.

So you can't really think that if we had sex, I'd say, Okay, I really expected a lot more than that. I changed my mind. It's over.

Yeah, but what if you're disappointed?

What do you mean?

I mean girls used to say I was fucking boring in bed.

How so?

Because I just wanted what I wanted. I didn't fucking care. I didn't go out of my fucking way to do anything for them.

But this would be different. Besides, you wouldn't have to do anything except cooperate. I would just want to have you there to enjoy in whatever way I wanted.

Why?

You want me to
get graphic?

No. I don't know.
I just mean . . .
you haven't even seen
me with my
clothes off except
for my shirt, unless
you spied on me or
something when I
didn't know it.

I saw you naked
once.

When?

You know when.
About a month
ago.

How?

You know how. I
walked by your

door for whatever reason, and it was open, and I wondered why you left it open, because you always shut it, and I looked inside, and you were naked.

Okay.

Yeah.

Doing what?

You remember what.

Okay, I remember.

So I've seen you.

So you know I'm no fucking big deal.

Honestly, I thought you looked hot.

Girls didn't think so.

Fuck girls. Anyway, how do you know?

I don't know. They never said anything. I'm not muscular or whatever.

Thank God.

Yeah, well, then why didn't you fucking come in? I fucking looked at you. You fucking knew. I could see that you knew.

You know what I thought? I thought you were feeling so depressed that you didn't care. To me, your eyes said, Fuck, here it is. You still want it, take it.

Exactly.

That's not the same thing as wanting it.

It is to me. When you didn't want it, it fucking killed me. I've never hated myself so much.

Do you know I went into the kitchen and got that big knife and

almost ran in your room and stuck it in your back? I was so frustrated and so turned on and so sick of you depriving me.

Yeah, I heard you in the kitchen.

What did you think?

I didn't think anything. I was scared that it was happening, and . . . I don't know, that I just . . . I was just fucking scared.

Me too. You should have seen me.

It's like I knew exactly how it would feel, and when I knew that, I wanted it. I was shaking and I couldn't breathe I wanted it so bad. Oh, fuck.

So what did it feel like?

I can't describe it. I'm not like you.

Maybe I should have done it.

When you didn't come back, I wanted to kill myself. I mean more than I ever have before. I felt so fucking hopeless and ugly and stupid. I

thought you saw
me, and then you
didn't want me.

**If I'd come back,
I would have
killed you.**

I would have let
you. God, you're
such a fucking
asshole.

Don't yell.

Fuck you, fuck
you, fuck you.
Don't you fucking
understand? Don't
you fucking get it?

**I think I get it. I
just can't believe
it.**

I fucking love you.
I don't want to
fucking live.

Okay, but don't you understand?

I don't fucking care.

I want you to love me. I almost killed you because you didn't. Because you were finally giving it to me, but it didn't mean anything because it didn't mean anything to you.

You didn't want it.

I did.

No, you wanted to kill me.

Because you didn't want it.

I did.

I wanted it, Chris.

Yeah, well, I know that now. You say that now. But you seem like you don't want it now.

I want it.

So what's the problem?

What do you think?

I think . . . Fuck, I think you kind of want it, but you don't really want it because I'm a useless piece of shit so it won't fucking mean anything.

You're not.

Bullshit. I mean thanks.

Sure. Don't be angry.

I need to do a shot. Where's my stuff?

It's right there.

Look, I have to say something.

What?

I'm just going to say this. I know this is pathetic, but . . . Do you love me or not? Because it seems like . . . you're kind of saying you do.

Why, what did I say?

Well, you said I'm cute and interesting and . . . you don't want to throw me out and you want to have sex with me and you don't want me to kill myself.

Yeah.

So . . . Oh, forget it. I don't fucking care. I just want to get high.

I agree that makes me sound like somebody who loves the person he's talking about.

Cool.

But I don't want to talk about it anymore.

I don't either. Let me do my shot.

I mean if I do, I do, and if I don't, I don't.

I don't care. Hold on a second.

I mean I probably do.

Whatever. Look, I love you. I want to have sex with you. I want you to love me, okay? But you're ruining my high, so please shut the fuck up.

BRIAN AKA "BEAR"

I spent the summer of 1969 vacationing with my family on the island of Maui. I was sixteen, and Bear was fifteen. He lived very near the beachfront hotel where we were staying and spent most of his mornings surfing the smallish, reliable waves that died on the sand a few yards below our balcony. Watching him became my daily routine, not because I liked surfing itself, much less his rather klutzy if patient style. He was the kind of boy I used to close my eyes, reach into my underwear, and build from scratch. To see Bear, track down a photo of the legendary skateboarding wunderkind Jay Adams when he was in his early teens. Take away Adams's grace, and Bear could have been his twin. One morning early in our vacation, my favorite surfer noticed the pale, slightly older boy studying him from a perch on the hotel and yelled for me to come down and share a joint. By the time he'd lit the second joint, Bear, who was as confident and blunt as I was shy and circuitous, had forced me to admit I was into him, and we were walking back to his place.

Bear was a jokey, class clown type who seemed lazily asexual in public, but, when alone and stoned, he was a sex maniac with the wildest imagination I'd ever encountered to that point. Nowadays there are labels for guys like him—"hungry, insatiable bottom" might begin to do the trick—but back then he seemed indescribable. I'd read about boys like him in novels, but the novels in question had been written by de Sade, and the characters in question were only slutty thanks to other characters' death threats. With Bear, it was almost nonstop sex the whole two months we spent together, both one-on-one and with a wide array of other young locals and tourists, quite a few of them otherwise straight guys disarmed by drugs and Bear's lean, persuasive body. We even had several incestuous S&M-ish three-ways with his thuggish older brother. He taught me a lot, instigated my lifelong fascination with rimming, and, even more than that, with young male asses in general, scarring my fantasies and fiction forever.

When I returned to LA at the end of summer, Bear and I exchanged pornographic letters for a while. There was even some back and forth about him running away to LA to live secretly in our "maid's quarters," as my parents joshingly referred to the disused, semi–storage room area over our garage. But then Bear started enthusing too much about all the crazy sex he could have with all my horny LA friends. For some reason, I had been thinking we'd be devoted boyfriends, so I changed the subject. Then one day Bear wrote to say he'd quit doing drugs and found Christ. There was no regret or backpedaling or recrimination in the message, just his casual announcement and a less lascivious than usual good-bye. It was okay with me by then because his body had been usurped by bodies more or less available to me. About two years later, I got an invitation to Bear's wedding accompanied by a touristy snapshot of him and the presumed bride standing in a comically tight hug on the same beach where he'd surfed.

THREE BOYS WHO THOUGHT
EXPERIMENTAL FICTION
WAS FOR PUSSIES

Scott's ass was almost too good to be true, like a professional cyclist's, despite the fact that his idea of exercise was refilling his bong. It was a genetic fluke, he told me, passed down through generations of boxy-assed relatives. In his jeans, it looked severe, like something best appreciated through binoculars, but once he'd gotten stoned enough to share, it was an unexpectedly soft, relaxed, and even gentle thing. A gym membership might have stabilized its muscles and polished its dazzling surface to an even more jaw-dropping stage, but

I doubt that perfect ass would have melted in one's mouth like Scott's did. Also, he had the deepest crack I've ever seen. Even with the lights on, it would have taken both my hands and a flashlight in my teeth to get to know it.

It's like Matthew's ass had finished growing at the age of eleven or twelve. So while the rest of him enlarged, it could only adjust, like a pair of size S underwear on a size L man. There wasn't much there if you need your asses to be classics, but if you see the butt as art, it was a James Turrell or Robert Ryman. When he walked, it trembled. When he bent down to scratch his foot, you could have tied a ball of string to it and started running down a beach. Its crack was just a crease that couldn't possibly disguise what it was there to protect. Luckily for him, his asshole was a Tiffany dead ringer with a lovely personality—winking, peering, squinting at anyone willing to spend his sweet time around it. Unlike his icy-eyed, tight-lipped, holier-than-thou, mathematically cute face.

I knew Rick's ass from porn films, but several years had passed, and it had slightly gone to seed. Still, it was very friendly, or maybe I mean more realistic. Superficially, it hadn't changed that much. Still, who knew what was happening inside? I was too afraid to ask. Its appetite for things too large and obviously painful hadn't changed, but what had once seemed impossible wasn't anymore, so when it gobbled up my fist that didn't make him a magician. He lay down on his stomach. I fisted him then crawled on top and fucked my brains out. Right before I came, he delivered a line of bad dialogue with such intensity it would have turned one of his porn scenes into a comedy. But I came because he meant it. "I wish your cock was eight feet long," he said. "God, I wish that."

THE WORST (1960–1971)

When I was nine, I visited my grandmother in Texas for a month during my summer vacation. She lived next door to a church, which played host to a big wedding one day. I walked over there by myself to watch the festivities. There was a blond girl about my age wearing a very frilly white dress standing on a walkway lined with burning tiki torches. I thought she was the most beautiful thing I'd ever seen. I was staring at her in awe when one of the tiki torches fell over, igniting her dress. Within a second, her whole body was consumed in fire. The next thing I remember was 48 hours later when a police officer found me in a state of shock hiding under my grandmother's house. I don't know if the girl lived or died.

When I was eleven, my friends and I were playing in the bushes in front of my house. We wanted to dig a hole, but I couldn't find a shovel in our storage room, so we decided to use an axe instead. A friend was chopping the ground into a hole when I unthinkingly crawled out of the bushes right where he was chopping. The axe went into the top of my head, splitting it wide open, and knocking me unconscious. My friends freaked out and left me there. I eventually regained consciousness, realized my head was gushing blood, reached up to feel what was wrong, and touched what I realized was my exposed brain. I ran to our front door screaming, and I was rushed to the hospital. The doctors saved my life, but I was bedridden and in extreme pain for months. The boy who axed me was so traumatized that he never looked me in the eyes or talked to me again. He killed himself at fifteen.

When I was thirteen, I wanted to be an archaeologist. My father knew a wealthy Peruvian man who financed archaeological digs, so I was sent down to Peru for the summer to stay with the man's family and work on the digs. To get to the site of the dig required me to take a long bus ride every day on a very old, scary, overcrowded bus. One day the bus came to a screeching halt in the middle of nowhere. The driver got up and walked past me into the back of the bus. When he returned he was carrying what looked like a passed-out male passenger. When he reached my seat, he stumbled, and the man he was carrying fell partly across my lap and the lap of the woman sitting next to me. That's when I realized the man was dead. He was cold and had an identifiably dead look on his face. The driver steadied himself, picked up the body, walked to the door of the bus, and threw the body out onto the side of the road. Then he got back in his seat and drove on. The other people in the bus acted like it was nothing, like it happened every day.

When I was fourteen, my mother ordered me to get a haircut. I refused and locked myself in the toilet of the little bathroom in my bedroom. I was in there for hours. Eventually, my father got home from work and kicked the door in. I ran into my bedroom with him chasing me, yelling at me, and whipping at me with his belt. I was really scared, so when I saw my mother standing in the doorway, I ran over and threw my arms around her, begging her to tell him to stop. Instead she grabbed my shoulders, turned me around, and held me tightly in place while my father whipped my face over and over with his belt. That was the moment I stopped trusting them.

When I was fifteen, my mother served my father with divorce papers then escaped with us kids to Maui, Hawaii, for two months. While there I made friends with a boy named Craig who had a huge supply of LSD. He and I took LSD twenty-four hours a day for the next month. I must have slept a little during that time, but I don't remember doing so. I became almost completely separated from reality. Occasionally, reality would fade back for a short time and I'd find myself walking somewhere I didn't recognize or talking to someone I didn't know, and then reality would disappear again. After a month of this, Craig and I were hitchhiking when some local Hawaiian guys picked us up. They drove us into a remote pineapple field and said they were going to kill us. Craig later told me they were joking, but I didn't think so at the time and completely freaked out. I was so freaked out that the Hawaiian guys ordered us out of the car and drove off. For the next eight or so hours, I had a massive nervous breakdown, screaming and convulsing and hallucinating violently while my friend watched over me. For months afterward, I was barely functional and could hardly speak, but I somehow managed to fly under the radar at home and at school.

When I was sixteen, my parents' ugly and prolonged divorce turned my mother into an extreme alcoholic for a couple of years. Every day held some unpredictable, terrifying behavior. Like she would come into the room where my siblings and I were watching TV, and, having drawn our attention, she'd put a handful of sleeping pills in her mouth. We would have to grab and wrestle her to the floor and force her to spit them out. She would stand at the top of the staircase in our house for hours begging one of us to come push her down the stairs and kill her. She'd gather us into the family car, start driving down the street at top speed, and aim at a wall or streetlight yelling, "I'm going to kill us all," and we'd have to grab the steering wheel from her and slam on the brakes. When she was really angry at us, she'd turn off all the electricity in the house, lock the fuse box so we couldn't turn the power back on, and start smashing furniture and things with an axe. Etc. Etc.

When I was seventeen, I went to a party where a bunch of my friends were hanging out. A few of them, including a guy named Dave, were getting high by shooting aerosol from altered paint cans into a paper bag and inhaling. They asked if I wanted to take a hit, and I said no. After I left the party, there was an accident. Somehow when Dave was shooting the aerosol into the bag, he filled the bag with paint instead. He inhaled the paint, which coated his lungs and suffocated him to death on the spot. My friends who were with him later told me it was the most horrible death you could imagine.

When I was eighteen, I was hanging out with my boyfriend Julian in Hollywood one afternoon while he worked as a street hustler. He was off turning a trick and I was talking to one of the other hustlers when this young hustler Julian and I knew pretty well, and with whom we'd had a three-way a couple of weeks previous, staggered up the sidewalk. We just thought he was really high so we started laughing and yelling jokey things at him, but when he got close to us he fell down and didn't move. We went over to him, and only realized then that he'd been stabbed numerous times in the back and was dead. We ran away in horror, and I later found out from another hustler that his body had lain there on the sidewalk for over three hours before anyone cared enough to call the police.

When I was eighteen, a friend of mine named David and I drove to the cool local record store. While we were shopping, this guy about our age came up to me and asked where I was going after leaving the store, then asked if he could catch a ride. He seemed okay, so I said sure. When we'd driven a few blocks, the guy pulled out a gun and put it to my head, telling me to pull over to the curb and that he was going to drive. As soon as we pulled over, my friend jumped out of the car and ran away. I gave the guy the wheel, and for next ten hours he drove all over the city with me as his hostage, picking up friends of his until the car was full of guys. It was basically a joyride. The guy would smash my car into parked cars for kicks, and they were all drinking heavily. At one point, I tried to escape, but they ran after me and dragged me back into the car. Finally, the guy stopped the car at a friend's house to buy drugs, and while he was out of the car, the other guys told me they'd let me go if I gave them all rides back to their respective houses. So I did, and the last guy I dropped off told me that if I told the police or if he ever saw me again, he'd kill me.

When I was eighteen, my uncle, who'd been a painter and therefore my hero when I was a little kid, but who'd later turned into an alcoholic womanizing leech who referred to me as "the pig," blew his brains out with a shotgun.

ONE NIGHT IN 1979 I DID TOO MUCH COKE AND COULDN'T SLEEP AND HAD WHAT I THOUGHT WAS A MILLION-DOLLAR IDEA TO WRITE THE DEFINITIVE TELL-ALL BOOK ABOUT GLAM ROCK BASED ON MY OWN PERSONAL EXPERIENCE BUT THIS IS AS FAR AS I GOT

It was 1972–73. There used to be this nightclub on Sunset Boulevard called Rodney Bingenheimer's English Disco where every star who was remotely Glam Rock—Bowie, Sparks, Roxy Music, T. Rex, Slade, Suzi Quatro, Jobriath, the Sweet, et al.—hung around when they were performing in town. I was just out of high school, and very "glammed" up—platforms, shag haircut, shimmery outfits, etc.—so I gravitated to the club, like wannabe cool people did. We danced, did a lot of quaaludes and downers, talked to Rodney, who was sweet but a moron, and waited for Glam celebs to show up. Then we'd schmooze them for whatever—jobs, drugs, ego boosts—and/or try to get in their pants. It was a serious contest. We even drew up this graph with a point system indicating which stars were the most trophy-like—Bowie, Bryan Ferry, Marc Bolan, Todd Rundgren, and I forget who else—all the way down to the "only when desperate" types—say Lou Reed, or the drummer from Silverhead, or any local band member, no matter how foxy and unknown, or how famous but unbelievably disgusting like Flo and Eddie, or how great but too old and insane like Arthur Lee. I wasn't that cute, obviously, but I was smarter than most of those overdressed airheads, so I was a top notch schmoozer, if a total loser as a groupie. Everyone who mattered dropped by Rodney's at some point. All the names: Paul Lynde, Andy Warhol, Erik Estrada, Debbie fucking Reynolds, Raymond fucking Burr. Even enemies of music like Jackson Browne and the Eagles. And since Glam was all about sex as rebellion and bisexual cool, stars treated the club like a brothel. Like I remember Bowie picked up one cute Glam boy whose name escapes me, tied him up, fucked him, then pissed all over him in a bathtub. Actually, his name was Karl. He played bass for a really well-known band of the time, and you can easily figure out his identity if you care. Fuck him. Several boys and girls did Iggy Pop, who was such a total junkie back then that he wasn't the trophy you would think. After a while, Iggy would stagger into the club yet again, and we'd just go, "Puh-lease." Anyway, one of the regulars was this very cute, pimply boy a little younger than me. Everyone was into him. His energy level was just adorable—I can't begin to do it justice—although a few years afterward when he became extremely famous, that same energy fueled one of the creepiest, most backstabbing personalities in the history of showbiz, if you ask me. Anyway, he's a joke dinner theater actor now, so ha ha. Point is, the energetic boy had a rock band, a kind of Tinkertoy Iggy and the Stooges meets something really horrible like, say, when the Bay City Rollers went heavy metal, if you remember that phase. One night they played at the club. They were so pathetic it was almost sublime. Here's this sixteen-year-old rich kid screaming suicidal threats, pretending to shoot up, and acting all wasted and animalesque. We were all just like, "Yum." After the show, he joined us at our table, which was extremely unusual. I guess he was tired. For a while in its history, Rodney's had these big round tables where regulars sat around strategizing and saying, like, "Look . . . yawn . . . it's the guitarist from Zolar X . . . yawn." So I was sitting at a table with Chuckie Starr—that's two r's—who was sort of famous at the time for wearing seven-foot platform shoes on *The Mike Douglas Show*, and this girl named Michelle, who was fucking Rod Stewart—in fact he wrote this famous song about her—I forget its title—that goes, "Red lips, hair, and fingernails / I hear you're a mean old Jezebel," and some other bullshit. She was there. And Sable Starr—again two r's—who ended up snagging Johnny Thunders, and even lived with him, which impressed us at the time, although, really, it can't have been all that much fun. There were all these other people too—nice, creepy, cute, not cute. Anyway, I was pontificating, like I tended to do, about how, say, the Raspberries' songs were so hermetic they were holy or something, and the energetic boy seemed impressed, but then he wasn't, like, brilliant. So our eyes started flashing back and forth. You know, that way. Lust. No one could believe it, because he seemed so unavailable. After a while, he said, "You should, um, come home with me." And I was, like, "Done. Say the word." So I drove him to his house—this big white mansion a block or two south of Sunset—and we snuck inside—it was about five in the morning—so as not to wake up his parents. But his mom was awake for some reason, I don't know why. I think she was a diet-pill head. Her eyes were really weird. She stopped us in the hallway. That's when I thought, "Oh my God." Because she was the star of this hugely famous TV series, which meant she was also the mother of this hugely famous teen idol/actor/singer of the period, which meant that the energetic boy was, like, royalty. I was thinking, "I fucking scored." Because he'd never exactly let on that he was you-know-who's little brother. Anyway, his mother, who's a Republican scumbag in real life, was actually nice. She didn't give a shit that we were completely 'luded out. She was just, like, "Have fun, you two." It must have been the diet pills talking. Then he and I went to his bedroom. We took some more quaaludes, and smoked some pot, and I forget what else, frankly—probably talked about his famous mother and brother—and I was beginning to see what a superficial little narcissist he was underneath all that cuteness. But at that point, who cared? And I think he eventually said, "Let's, you know, do it." Not an exact quote. And we took off our clothes, and then . . . it's all sort of hazy, I guess because of the drugs. But we did all the obvious stuff, and I remember that at one particular point I had been rimming him for, like, an hour, as I tended to do, especially when I was on downers, and thinking, "Wow, he must really love to be rimmed," and "We were made for each other," etc. I looked up, because I needed another hit of his face to stay interested, and that's when I realized that the look on his face, which I'd been reading as slack-faced delirium, as, "Oh, I have found the sublime," or "Oh Dennis, how could I have lived so long without . . . etc.," or whatever, had nothing to do with me. He'd been asleep the whole time, the self-involved little piece of shit. Yeah, like that stopped me.

THE NOLL DYNASTY

Kip Noll (late '70s to early '80s)

Patriarch of the Noll clan. Arguably the most famous gay porn star of his era. His popularity paved the way for the "twink" performers who dominate gay porn today. Displayed reasonable, Steve McQueen–like acting skills. Versatile top, occasional bottom.

Plusses: Surfer/skateboarder image, finger-snap erections, tough but laid-back demeanor, dick.

Minuses: Receding hairline, emotionally detached, clock-puncher, too often miscast as a top.

Jeff Noll (late '70s)

The first porn star to milk Kip's fame by adopting his surname. Billed as Kip's younger brother. His oeuvre consists of a single scene in one film misleadingly titled *Jeff Noll's Buddies*. Nonetheless, he has a cult following to this day. Bottom.

Plusses: The technically cutest Noll, unique facial expressions when fucked, ass, nipples, legs.

Minuses: Bent dick, emotionally detached, too brief career.

Bob Noll (late '70s)

Billed as Kip's hunky older brother. Didn't manage to parlay the Noll name into much of a career. Appeared in one feature film, *Street Boys*, and several solo jack-off shorts. Top.

Plusses: Genuinely hunky if you like that type, eyes, dick, inexplicably sympathetic.

Minuses: Too obviously a straight guy paid to do a gay guy's job, emotionally detached, sluggish.

Marc Noll (late '70s)

Billed as Kip's cousin. Like Jeff and Bob, he had a brief career, appearing in one film, *The Adventures of Marc Noll*. While the fates and/or current whereabouts of the other early Nolls are unknown, Marc is known to have drowned in his bathtub in the mid-'80s. Bottom.

Plusses: Slightly less emotionally detached, slutty, stoner jock image, lips.

Minuses: Performed visibly drunk, an okay but not remarkable body, only cute from certain angles.

Scott Noll (late '70s to early '80s)

Billed as Kip's other younger brother. The first Noll to bear absolutely no physical resemblance to Kip. Appeared in three films: *The Summer of Scott Noll*, *Cuming of Age*, and *Flashback*, costarring with Kip in the latter two titles. Appeared to be the last of the Noll lineage until Chip's arrival fifteen years later.

Plusses: The sexiest and best performer of the bunch, ballet dancer posture, piggy bottom, ass, eyes, eager to please.

Minuses: Seemed very dumb, emotionally detached, visible discomfort when kissing.

Chip Noll (late '90s to ?)

Initially billed as Kip's nephew. The most prolific and arguably successful Noll. Has appeared in roughly two dozen feature length videos. Mysteriously disappeared from the business for three years in the early '00s, then made a mysterious comeback to star in a dozen plus more videos. Bottom.

Plusses: Piggy bottom, flirt, nose, eyes, Superman logo tattoo, varied roles (from army private to queeny skater to S&M slave).

Minuses: Occasional anal wart, emotionally detached, snooty attitude, post-comeback body thickness.

THE FIFTEEN WORST RUSSIAN GAY PORN WEB SITES

`Spankingforest.com`
Apparently there's a Russian forest where teens hang out, but unfortunately there's an ugly fat old guy who hangs out there too and for some reason when they see him they let him spank them.

`Justmarriedgays.com`
To believe this site, when Russian gay couples get married, one of them dresses in drag, then they have an orgy with a few of their ugliest friends.

`Gayschief.com`

Even though Gay's Chief's office is just a desk in the middle of an empty room, the job he's offering pays so well that boys will swallow his cum to get it.

`Gay-lessons.com`

The twinks starring on this site don't know how to have sex, so a much older, unattractive guy shows them how to do it, and we get to watch.

`Boyknights.com`

This magical Russian site has a time machine that whisks its photographer back to the medieval period, when gay sex was as common as the housefly.

`Studsfun.com`

Two of Russian porn's most ubiquitous models run a cross-dressing site where they lure straight studs back to their pad and shock the studs gay with their permanently flaccid penises.

`Drunkengay.com`

This site is unique because its models are actual burnt-out, overweight young alcoholics who have listless, sluggish sex the way real hopeless drunks probably do.

`Daddysonfuck.com`

Like every other intergenerational site, this one promises real incest, and even though simple logic is enough to scotch that claim, its forbidden lovers do look like products of the same unpleasant gene pool, so, on that level only, thumbs-up.

Theyyoung.com

Notable for heavily employing buzz magnet model du jour Rostik, aka "Justlike Timberlake," and for hosting a nice-try *Rocky Balboa*–like comeback by the disturbingly catatonic, glassy-eyed, leathery former superstar Ton.

Madonboys.com

To what lengths would you have to go to suck in members when your site is the thousandth one showing cute-ish late-teen boys sucking cock and fucking in an abysmally furnished Russian living room?

Popupboys.com

This site get points from me for the fact that one of its models looks like the guy who would stand in front of Mann's Chinese Theater pretending to Vincent Kartheiser if Vincent Kartheiser were a big star.

Badcowboys.com

Clues that this is not an American-owned site: (1) They don't care if there weren't cars with Ukrainian license plates in the 1800s. (2) They use the word "cute" the way we use the word "the." (3) Their membership costs $39.95 a month, and it cannot be canceled.

Strokemycock.com

Do you remember that scene in *The Basketball Diaries* where Leonardo DiCaprio's character gets a blow job in a toilet stall, and from his facial expression you'd think he was simultaneously being punched in the stomach and watching his mother's head be cut off? Did you think maybe he was overacting just a little? Well, once you see the misery and horror these Russian twinks feel upon being masturbated, you might think differently.

Siberianboys.com

In the old Russia, Siberia was a cold, remote part of the country where criminals were sent to spend the rest of their obscure lives in ramshackle gulags. In the new Russia, it's where gullible American and European gays pay to watch the same ten or so models do outdoors the same few things they do indoors on forty other Russian porn sites.

Guyfoot.com

Not being a foot fetishist, I can't prove that the foot-inclined don't show their lust and appreciation by holding ankles, toes, etc. an inch away from their faces, then scrunching their eyes shut and opening their mouths as wide as possible, but it seems like a decent guess.

THE ASH GRAY PROCLAMATION

Mackerel lives in a lower-class suburb of Pawheen, Arkansas. He's thirteen years old and wears his dirty hair long. He wanted to be an architect when he grew up. Then he got stoned yesterday and paid a psychic to tell him the truth. According to the spirits, he'll be dead from a drug overdose within forty-eight hours. Having been molested by half the town's male population, Mackerel is something of a pragmatist. So he's embraced an early death with a young teen's impatience. At the moment, he sits on his bike finessing dope off some sixteen-year-old junkie named Josh who lifts weights and has a trendy short haircut.

JOSH (*impatiently*): If you want my advice, cut your vocal cords out. It's a simple operation. Otherwise you're so awesome, it's scary.

MACKEREL: Thanks, but I'm looking for dope.

JOSH (*darkly*): Thank my uncle. You don't even want to know.

MACKEREL: Know what?

JOSH: That we're gay boyfriends, you idiot. I don't know why we moved out here from LA. You're all retarded.

MACKEREL: Thank him for what?!

Mackerel kicks one of his bike pedals angrily and it spins. Josh watches the pedal revolve until his eyes are wide with staring.

MACKEREL: I'm smart enough to know you're just like everyone else in this stupid town who wants my ass, but I don't care anymore.

JOSH (*vacantly*): If you want to ask me something, do it now, because I think I'm hypnotized.

Mackerel snaps his fingers in Josh's blank face.

MACKEREL: Okay, do you want my ass or not?

JOSH: No, my uncle does. And he doesn't want it. He wants me to want it. I mean he wants me to have it first. So it's a trial run. But he's the one who has a thing for you. And he's not really my uncle. So, no, not technically.

MACKEREL: You lost me. But that's cool.

Josh: He wants to be a cannibal. You should hear him talk about me. I'm a junkie, or I'd leave him.
Mackerel: It's weird, but I saw that happening in a dream. I think I'm psychic.
Josh: I dream all the time. Heroin's great.
Mackerel (*angrily*): Then give me some. Jesus.
Josh: I need to buy a gun.

Mackerel climbs off his bike and starts undoing his belt. One of his ankles accidentally hits the spinning pedal, which stops it dead.

Josh: Oh, shit. I was just hypnotized, wasn't I?
Mackerel: Here, do it and tell your boyfriend about me. Anything you want.

Mackerel lays his bike down on the sidewalk, which requires him to bend so far over it pulls his baggy jeans tight.

Josh: God, you have, like, no ass.
Mackerel: Hey, I'm fucking thirteen. What do you expect?
Josh: No, I mean I finally get the whole pedophile thing. Wow, it's addictive.

Ten minutes later, Mackerel is in an uncomfortable squat in some nearby bushes, and Josh is on his hands and knees sniffing around in Mackerel's crack like some dog.

Mackerel: Dude, hey, gay boy. You're obsessed. But don't stop.

JOSH: It's the illegality.

MACKEREL: And what else?

JOSH: That your ass is so nowhere. It's so flimsy and warm it's like an optical illusion. God, listen to me.

MACKEREL: I love it when you breathe out.

JOSH: Having sex with a thirteen-year-old. Who'd have thought? It's like I finally know myself.

MACKEREL: You mean you know me. Not to be egomaniacal.

JOSH: So you're an anarchist. That's hot too.

MACKEREL: I try. But I'm only thirteen, so it's all just a theory.

JOSH: You're God. I just figured it out.

MACKEREL: Maybe to you. I mean I wish.

JOSH: Seriously. You have to smell you. Use your fingers.

Mackerel dips a finger in his ass, then pulls it out and gives the tip a very tentative sniff.

MACKEREL: Hm.

JOSH: What did I tell you?

MACKEREL: I am God, aren't I? Weird.

JOSH: Yeah, well, just don't tell anyone. Otherwise, I'll never get laid.

MACKEREL: It smells like every other ass in the world, only much, much better. That's a guess.

JOSH: Well, duh. Being gay is the truth. You ought to try it. Oh, shit, I'm going to come.

MACKEREL: Knock yourself out. Oh, shit, me too.

Fifteen minutes later, Mackerel's lower legs have started aching, so he's on his hands and knees. Josh has gotten hard again, and alternates between rimming Mackerel and probing his ethereal ass with a finger.

MACKEREL: Just give me some heroin. What's your problem?
JOSH: You are.
MACKEREL: That's why I don't care if I die. If one more guy does this to me, I'm going to freak. My blood pressure's insane.
JOSH: You should charge.
MACKEREL: I do. Money's not my problem. Beauty is. It's weird. I used to be no one for years.
JOSH: If you can hold out until you're middle-aged, you'll be no one again. You should see my quote-unquote uncle.
MACKEREL: Thanks, but death calls. That sounded more ominous than it feels.
JOSH: I would have paid you a hundred thousand dollars to do this. But I'm horny so don't quote me.
MACKEREL: That would have worked.
JOSH: I mean I would have if I had it. Maybe my quote-unquote uncle has it. He certainly acts like he's rich. He bought me from the straight world in so many words.
MACKEREL: What do you guys do in bed? Not that I care.
JOSH: This. Only I'm you, and he's every guy who's ever done this to you, if you catch my drift. He also fistfucks me. And he pretends to cook me in the fireplace, and then pretends to carve me into steaks and eats them. I guess they're steaks.

They're invisible, so how would I know?

MACKEREL: What do you mean by fistfuck?

JOSH: What do you mean by what do I mean? It's self-explanatory. Why do you care?

MACKEREL: Because it keeps coming up in conversation. Well, not conversation, because I never say anything back. It must be a fad.

JOSH: I love you.

MACKEREL: Yeah, that word keeps coming up too.

JOSH: I want to protect you from the world, and give you anything you want. I can't believe it.

MACKEREL: Ditto. I mean everyone says that too.

Ten minutes later, Josh is finally bored of sex, and the two boys are sitting side by side on some grass.

JOSH (*mournfully*): I'm no one now. I've gone from being you to being whoever.

MACKEREL: I'll be dead in a couple of days, if that helps. Besides, I make everyone depressed. Being God sucks.

JOSH: Being the ex-God sucks worse. I should just let my boyfriend eat me. Who cares anymore?

MACKEREL (*impatiently*): Tell me more about me. God commands you.

JOSH: Well, this is more about me than it is about you, but I'll be happy when you're dead and unattractive.

MACKEREL: That's about me.

JOSH: Then there you go.

MACKEREL: You just need to have sex with somebody who'll never ever have me no matter how much they beg. And I know just the guy, unless you're racist. He's from Bin Laden-ville.
JOSH: Like I care. Like who does it to me ever has an identity.
MACKEREL: I hear that.
JOSH: Is he cute? Not that I care what guys look like.
MACKEREL: I'm a racist. So you tell me.
JOSH: Bin Laden's cute.

Mackerel grabs his stomach and gags.

MACKEREL: Then he's cute. God, ugh, that's disgusting. I'm going to throw up.

About an hour later, Mackerel, Josh, and the aforementioned psychic are sitting in a circle on an old Persian rug in the latter's little storefront. He's just finished reading Josh's tarot cards. Since the psychic is a Middle Easterner, it feels realistic.

JOSH (*to the psychic*): Quit staring at my crotch.
PSYCHIC: Crotch smotch.
MACKEREL (*to the psychic*): He's freaked out. He needs more heroin.
PSYCHIC: I don't care.
MACKEREL (*to Josh*): Reality isn't reality to a psychic. I'm pretending he's a painting.
JOSH: I've never seen a painting. That's like paint on something flat that looks exactly like a picture, right? Like I care.

MACKEREL: Not really. It's better. It's even more real in a weird way. Like *Tony Hawk's Pro Skater 3* on pause, but more serene.

Josh thinks about that until he seems satisfied.

JOSH (*to the psychic*): Okay, we're cool if you can channel my ugly, middle-aged boyfriend. 'Cos he's my problem.

Hearing that, the psychic shuts his eyes, bows his head, and becomes a kind of human speakerphone.

PSYCHIC (*in a gay-sounding voice*): I want to eat you. Literally.
MACKEREL (*to the psychic*): I think my buddy knows that, but he wants to know the reason.
JOSH: When you're on heroin, you can calm down just like this.

He indicates how relaxed his whole body seems all of a sudden.

JOSH: Being a junkie is awesome.
MACKEREL (*to the psychic*): Can a thirteen-year-old be gay? I've always wondered.
PSYCHIC (*in a gay-sounding voice*): Oh my God, yes. Just let me eat my boyfriend, and we'll talk.
MACKEREL (*to Josh*): Now you ask him something.

Josh sits there thinking angrily for a minute.

JOSH: Okay, if you eat me, what will happen? I mean on a universal level. I don't mean the temporary things like pain.

PSYCHIC (*in a gay-sounding voice*): This is nice. It's like we're going to a couple's counselor.

JOSH (*to Mackerel*): See, that's why I love my boyfriend. I need a father.

MACKEREL: Me too. It's weird.

PSYCHIC (*in a gay-sounding voice*): If I eat you, your life will have more implications. You won't just be hot and sixteen and a junkie. They'll write a book about you, or two or three books. People will always want to know why some gay guy would eat you.

Josh laughs delightedly.

JOSH (*to Mackerel*): That's so him.

Just then the psychic's head lifts and his beady eyes reopen. Mackerel and Josh look at him suspiciously.

PSYCHIC (*dazedly*): It's just erased time for me. But I don't care if you believe me or not.

MACKEREL (*to Josh*): We'd better pay him and go. I know him. But I'll say no more.

PSYCHIC (*to Josh*): Before I moved here from Afghanistan, I saw your ass in a dream.

JOSH: That's . . . nice?

The psychic whips his tunic off over his head and tosses it aside. His body is fleshy, bordering on obese, but shows signs of having been very well built at one time.

JOSH: Afghanistan is where heroin comes from, right?
PSYCHIC: Yeah, why?
MACKEREL (*to the psychic*): He's a junkie. We told you that when you were in that trance. But I'll say no more.
PSYCHIC: You know what's saddest about the world since 9/11? Even sadder than your dead and our dead?
JOSH: If it's not about heroin, I don't care. Well, heroin or my boyfriend. Fuck, I wish I understood why we love, don't you? I mean we humans. I would have been a movie star by now. That was my old goal.
PSYCHIC: You're sexy when you're thoughtful.
JOSH: Pshaw. But that's sweet.
PSYCHIC: You would have been a whore. You'll be one anyway. That's foretold by that card over there. I just tell it like it is. I can't care about your feelings. You want some heroin? I could use some too.
JOSH: Sure. I don't care about my boyfriend when I'm loaded.

The psychic pulls a packet of yellowy quote-unquote dope out of his discarded tunic.

PSYCHIC: Not to put too fine a point on it, but the thing about the 9/11 bullshit? It wasn't Bin Laden. It wasn't even Al Qaeda.

JOSH: I know. It was our hearts.
PSYCHIC (*with irritation*): Somebody should murder you.
JOSH: Heroin is murder.

The psychic tosses Josh the quote-unquote dope, then appears to lose his preternatural Islamic-style mystery and cool.

PSYCHIC (*angrily*): No, really murder you. I mean as soon as possible. Like now, hint hint. If we were in Afghanistan, everyone would want to murder you. You wouldn't last a day. Your stupid American morality is why we hate you and want to live here and hate living here. But you need psychics.
JOSH: You're good.
PSYCHIC: I'm not that good. I'm just ambitious. But you call that terrorism.
JOSH: You think I don't understand you, but I can. Guys have pulled every kind of crap to get my ass. The murder thing is really, really old.
PSYCHIC: Then what did I just say? Either one of you boys feel free to answer, because I'd love to know what you think you know.
JOSH: Then read my mind. Or read his mind. Yeah, read his. I already know what I'm thinking.

The psychic glances meaningfully at Mackerel.

PSYCHIC: I can only read the future. And Mackerel doesn't have one. But he and I have been through this already.

JOSH: Okay, then how does his future not happen? If you're so fucking brilliant.
PSYCHIC: Do that dope. Learn by example.
JOSH: That's a thought. But still . . .
PSYCHIC: Okay, you think I'm attracted to you, right? I make you think that. It's an Afghan thing. That's how we bombed your fucking country. There's your proof.

Josh studies the psychic for a second, then laughs, and starts pouring the quote-unquote dope out on this little mirror he always carries around in his pocket just in case.

JOSH: You're good. I mean you're really, really good. Okay, you win. What are you into?
PSYCHIC: I'm into you not knowing what to expect. Okay, I'm into rimming and fistfucking. But do that dope first. I like my whores brain-dead.

Josh is already dividing the quote-unquote dope into lines with this razor blade he also carries with him.

JOSH (*distractedly*): Sounds good. I mean whatever you said.
PSYCHIC: In Afghanistan, there's very famous canyon called Khakistarikhan. It's the deepest canyon in all the world. When I'm through with you, I'm going to enter your ass in the Khakistarikhan look-alike contest. It's a big event in Islam, and you'll definitely win.

Josh (*to Mackerel*): If you'd ever been fistfucked, you'd be so turned on right now.
Mackerel: No, I wouldn't.
Psychic (*to Mackerel*): You should develop your gift. Let me have sex with your dead buddy here. Then I'll lend you a book.
Mackerel: According to you, I won't have time to read it.
Psychic: That's true, but don't make me laugh. I'll lose my focus. Here, junkie. Use this capitalist prop.

He hands Josh a hundred dollar bill. Josh rolls the bill into a straw, then leans over and snorts up all the quote-unquote dope.

Josh: Tell me more about this canyon. I mean more about me.
Psychic: Once a year, a huge prehistoric creature that lives deep in the canyon comes to the surface and does a little dance. He looks exactly like my forearm.
Josh: Whatever that means. Wow, this is killer heroin. I mean literally. I can feel the legend.

Josh has started to look too relaxed to be around a Middle Easterner in this political climate.

Mackerel (*to Josh*): Don't you see what he's doing? This is how the whole 9/11 bullshit happened. He just told you that himself.
Psychic (*to Mackerel*): He's beyond you. Besides, you love it.

MACKEREL: That could be true. I'd have to think about it.
PSYCHIC (*to Mackerel*): Don't you realize it yet? You're the one who wants a sixteen-year-old corpse. I'm just a nice guy.
MACKEREL: You're wrong.

He points down at the bulge in his blue jeans.

MACKEREL: This hard-on is bullshit. I just have this whole thing about overdosing on heroin. You started it. Sex is just like whatever. Dying is sex to me.
PSYCHIC: You're too good for this world. As opposed to that corpse or impending corpse over there. You knew him. So you tell me. Dead or not dead?

Mackerel glances at Josh and sees an ugly whitish color that has to mean death's in the mix, then starts rubbing his crotch to help counteract the unsexiness of his moral dilemma.

MACKEREL (*somberly*): He's history. We're like historians now.
PSYCHIC: Now I'll tell you the truth. I'm not just a psychic. I'm an Al Qaeda operative. He's my mission. It's all about semantics. Do you want to hear the story? It'll curl your toes.
MACKEREL: They already are. Maybe I'm psychic, because I already know what you're going to say.
PSYCHIC: I'm listening.
MACKEREL: If I tell you, you'll lose your hard-on. But you're a stalker. How's that for proof?

PSYCHIC: I love him. That's where our cultural differences get in the way. In my culture, this is love if you're gay. We're not fancy about it. You think we live in caves because we like to live in caves? It's a metaphor. We live together in caves until we find our own caves and fly away. I searched your country coast to coast, and this junkie's ass is mine. Wait'll you see it.
MACKEREL: Like you've seen it.
PSYCHIC: I didn't have to. That's just your literal American thinking. Don't even try to understand it.
MACKEREL: You're big on words and concepts. If I were gay, I'd say God is sex, and seducing straight boys like me is the prayer. Josh told me his boyfriend had to rob a bank to make him gay. He said before then he was just another guy who couldn't make the football team and turned into a stoner. Maybe he was lying, I don't know. The past isn't my thing. So I question your story. How's that for being psychic?
PSYCHIC: Maybe if I knew myself better, I'd agree. Your freedoms are intimidating. How's that for honesty?
MACKEREL: No offense. All I'm saying is your quest is nothing special. You and him are just porn. Death is sex. I mean my death, not his.
PSYCHIC: So I should murder you too? I'm confused.
MACKEREL: No, I'm just saying we should film it. Let's say, hypothetically, I film you doing gay stuff to him. Then we upload the video onto a Web site, and charge guys to watch. They jack off and imagine they're you and all that. Then at the end of the tape we put a little text that says, "Oh, by the way, the boy you just saw getting fucked and et cetera was dead, ha

ha ha. You're a necrophiliac. Busted." It might be like flying a plane into the World Trade Center, except a lot more profitable for us.

The psychic scrunches up his face in concentration for a moment.

PSYCHIC (*laughing*): I wonder who would win in a debate, Bin Laden or you? I'll always wonder that.

MACKEREL: You really need to chill on the Bin Laden thing. I mean if you guys over there in Afghanistan really want to be like the West.

PSYCHIC: I sort of wish he were alive. I mean the junkie, not Bin Laden. Don't get your hopes up. I just mean I wish he knew how much his ass will change the world. But I'm into S&M, so fuck him.

MACKEREL: Not to disappoint you, but his ass is kind of hairy. Not that I've seen it. You could shave it, I guess. We do that a lot over here.

PSYCHIC (*angrily*): That's so typically nihilistic of your culture.

MACKEREL: Here, I'll show you. It's not a trick. You could do it too, for future reference.

Mackerel tugs on one of the legs of Josh's jeans until there's a naked foot of calf, and rubs one finger gently through its modest thicket of blondish-brown hairs.

MACKEREL: See that? That's how you know.

PSYCHIC: I don't believe you. You're just superstitious. I know all about superstition. When you're poor and live in the desert you think all kinds of crazy shit.

MACKEREL: You want to bet? You'll lose, though.

PSYCHIC (*laughing*): Sometimes I forget you're only thirteen years old. Sure, I'll bet. What's the wager?

MACKEREL: Okay, if it's hairy, there's no God. And if it's smooth, there is.

PSYCHIC: How about if it's smooth, you can rim for a second. It had better be. In Afghanistan, it's a sea of hairy asses. That's why we're all pedophiles.

MACKEREL: Maybe I'm wrong, but with these calves, it would be a miracle. Anyway, to us a hairy sixteen-year-old ass is exotic. I've never even seen one.

PSYCHIC: Wait, what's the bet again?

MACKEREL: If I'm right, you'll give me enough of that heroin to kill me, and if I'm wrong, there's no God. But let's just do this fucking thing and move on to something else that we agree on like my future.

They lay Josh on his back, grab his blue jeans by the belt loops and yank them down over his knees, dragging a pair of jockey shorts along with them. Then they roll him over.

MACKEREL: Okay, that's weird. It's not only smooth. It's also perfectly shaped, if one knows anything about physics. I wasn't just wrong. I'm also gay, or gay for him, or gay for it. I don't know about him yet.

PSYCHIC: Stop apologizing and pray.

He kneels down, spreads Josh's cheeks, and starts licking and chewing dead ass crazily like he's a lion and it's attached to some gazelle.

MACKEREL: FYI, we call that rimming in the States because we know God is bullshit. But don't stop.

PSYCHIC: That's strange. We call this praying in Afghanistan because we know God is shit. Let me clarify. His shit. Or rather guys who look like him's shit. You'd qualify.

MACKEREL: That's your fucked-up trip. I'm still at the being-rimmed stage. Shit's for grown-ups.

PSYCHIC: Did you ever know this boy Steve? Blond, nineteen, quit school, converted to Islam, joined the Taliban, blah blah blah?

MACKEREL: Why would I? Unless he tried to turn me on to pot once. Read my mind, but keep rimming him too. Can you do that? We can.

The psychic shuts his eyes and concentrates.

PSYCHIC: That's him. Now read mine.

Mackerel shuts his eyes and concentrates.

MACKEREL: Jesus, I'm so gay. That's Steve Rosenberg, all right. What a great fucking ass. It makes mine seem like the Titanic.

PSYCHIC: Steve's ass even turned the great Bin Laden gay for an hour. Don't be so hard on yourself. In Afghanistan, Steve's ass is a national icon.

MACKEREL: And I could have had him. I'm an idiot. Tell me everything about Steve's ass, but keep rimming the dead guy.

PSYCHIC: In Afghanistan, when you want to give a cook the highest compliment there is, you use a phrase. I can't translate it. But it's something like, "Thank you for letting Steve sit on my face." Don't quote me.

MACKEREL: Your thoughts are terrorism.

PSYCHIC: Well, this junkie's ass makes Steve's ass taste irrelevant. And it's already cold. Imagine if I hadn't overdosed him. I'm such a rush-to-judgment type.

MACKEREL: Fine, Jesus, then scooch over a little.

He kneels beside the psychic, and starts rimming Josh too. His technique is a lot more romantic.

MACKEREL: Can you believe I've never done this?

PSYCHIC: No.

MACKEREL: I wonder how I'd rate? I mean if my ass were this ass, and you were me or whatever.

PSYCHIC: Some things are too beautiful to know. That's why I've never read Proust.

MACKEREL: So how was Steve compared to Proust?

PSYCHIC: I can only speculate. I'll just say that this writer friend of mine who rimmed Steve is called the Proust of Afghanistan by our literary establishment, such as it is. Before my friend had Steve, he wrote thrillers.

MACKEREL: I want to be rimmed. I mean again. I mean by Bin Laden or you.

PSYCHIC: Like I said.

MACKEREL: You and Steve seem like you were really good friends. But I'm gay so I don't care about friendship anymore. It's lame. Rimming is the truth. Hold his asscrack wider open so I can really eat his hole.

The psychic spreads the asscheeks helpfully and leans back to observe.

PSYCHIC: I could watch you do that all day.

MACKEREL: Me too, if I could.

PSYCHIC: By the way, this is jihad, if you care. You guys thought it was those planes. If Bin Laden is astral projecting himself into my body right this second—and if he isn't dead, he is—he's seriously digging what we're doing. I'm so going to heaven.

MACKEREL: That's debatable.

PSYCHIC: No, it's not. Anyway, it's been a second.

He knocks Mackerel out of the way, and goes down hard on Josh's ass.

MACKEREL (*angrily*): Friends don't do that. So we aren't friends. I don't know what to call this, though. We like categories over here.

PSYCHIC: So do we, but our categories are gigantic.

MACKEREL: See, we respect death too much. That's the only category that's gigantic over here. We're not like you.

PSYCHIC: So now you know.

He starts eating Josh out even more hungrily than before. The ass starts shaking and rocking from side to side and inflating and deflating like lungs.

MACKEREL: I'm bored.

PSYCHIC: I don't know that term.

MACKEREL: Boredom is what we call knowledge over here. The idea is that you never quite quote-unquote know, you just stop caring if you quote-unquote know. That's when you know.

PSYCHIC: Sounds interesting.

He lifts his head up for a moment and looks sincerely at Mackerel.

PSYCHIC: I mean that. You're a beautiful kid. I'm just—

MACKEREL: I know. I have to get out of here anyway. I've got a date with that wannabe cannibal guy. I just wanted to see you fistfuck him. It's so notorious.

PSYCHIC: I'll page you.

MACKEREL: Yeah, if I'm not food by then.

He crosses his fingers.

PSYCHIC: Page me when you're food. If I don't page you first. Or put paging me in your will. I'm just saying I care about you.
MACKEREL (*angrily*): Then give me some heroin. Jesus Christ, what does it fucking take?

A half hour later, Mackerel is sitting cross-legged on some grass in the town's little central park talking directly to you readers. He still isn't stoned, and there's a vibe of desperation in his voice.

MACKEREL (*dourly*): Hey, you want the cutest piece of ass you've ever had in your lives? I mean cutest for you, not for me. I happen to hate my good looks in a complicated way. Anyway, I'll trade you.
YOU: Thanks for spending time with us. You're God, et cetera, and we love your stupid Arkansas accent. Meaning yes.
MACKEREL: I even scream with an Arkansas accent. You'll love that too.
YOU: What's the trade? We're so damned horny.
MACKEREL: Don't rush me. I'm not like Josh. I need to get to know things before I do them.
YOU: At least take off your shirt.
MACKEREL: There's a trick to being me. It's called "who the fuck are you to ask?" When I'm shirtless, you'll know it.
YOU: Then make us hard.
MACKEREL: You already are. All it takes is my face. I think my haircut helps too. Long hair's back. But I guess when you're a pedophile, any kid is porn. Correct me if I'm wrong.

YOU: What do you like to do in bed? We mean what is "fuck" to you?

MACKEREL: Shooting heroin. Next?

YOU: Junkies are so boring. If you weren't thirteen, we wouldn't be here. We'd be in Thailand.

MACKEREL (*laughing*): Next. This is awesome. I was never loved when I was straight. So I'm drunk on your gayness. If you weren't here, I'd be in school or prison.

YOU: The world's a bar when we're with you. If you were old enough to be officially gay, you'd realize that's gay for "we love you." A thirteen-year-old skinny blond boy drunk in an Arkansas gay bar, Jesus. Let's play truth or dare.

MACKEREL: Cool. I like you so far. Okay, you earned it.

He whips off his T-shirt, and hurls it away.

YOU: Truth. By the way, you have the world's most perfect little ashtrays . . . we mean nipples.

MACKEREL: Okay, do you have any heroin? And before you say that's cheating, Kant says truth lies in the question one asks in pursuit of the truth. Actually, Buddha said that too. So now you know me. Oh, and thanks for the compliment, you liars. Dare.

YOU: We dare you to explain your intellect. You're thirteen. You quit school at eleven. Your foster parents chained you to a bunk bed at night. You're dyslexic. You're cute. So how the hell do you do it?

MACKEREL: I'm like a parrot. Literally, it's a serious condition. Parrot syndrome. Look it up. Plus I'm psychic and you're not. Truth.

You: Okay, we have enough heroin in our pockets to kill you a hundred times over. And clean works.

Mackerel: Duh.

He points to his temple.

Mackerel: I'm a psychic, you remember? But don't you wish this were a loaded gun?

You (*thoughtfully*): Hm.

Mackerel: I don't like the sound of that.

You: Us neither. Even thirteen-year-olds get old apparently. Who'd have thought?

Mackerel: Then give me all your heroin. God, I hate fags. We're all manipulative and shit. You have fifteen seconds to hand it over.

He looks at his watch.

You: And we can eat you out?

Mackerel: Yes.

You: And fistfuck you? Bondage, torture, videotape it, kill you when we're done with you?

Mackerel: Yes, yes, yes. Jesus Christ, are you deaf?

Mackerel takes all your heroin and works, then runs away without keeping his part of the bargain. Because you exist in the rational world, you have to watch his perfect ass fade away into the background and form a disconsolate circle jerk. The sky over Arkansas picks up on your vibes and grows silvery dark like one-way glass. On the other side of it, God's jerking off. The hicks think weather abnormalities are a sign that Armageddon has arrived and decide to rape their kids before they die. Mackerel rides his bike through streets filled with children's lustful screams. He eventually stops at Josh's boyfriend's house and falls into your trap. You're on the phone with Josh's boyfriend when Mackerel rings his front doorbell, so you let Mackerel go on one condition. Josh's boyfriend is short, ugly, but has clearly spent time in a gym, so he's hot to other gay guys.

JOSH'S BOYFRIEND (*startled*): Hey, I know you. Or maybe I wish I knew you. I don't know if you're gay, but crystal meth will do that.

MACKEREL: I just turned gay a few minutes ago, so don't ask me. Gee, Josh said you were even uglier, not that I care.

JOSH'S BOYFRIEND: I get uglier during sex. But thank God for what you see. Guess how old I am? Seriously, take a guess.

MACKEREL: Head-wise, I'd say, oh, mid-fifties, and body-wise, oh . . . late thirties tops. We gay guys have it all figured out, don't we?

JOSH'S BOYFRIEND: Being gay myself, it's impossible to say. One hears tales, though. My neighbor's super ugly, unless you like them fat and straight.

MACKEREL: I love everyone equally. Thank the shitload of heroin somewhere in your house. If it wasn't there, you'd be alone. Oh, your boyfriend's dead, by the way. I forgot. I'm the new guy.

JOSH'S BOYFRIEND (*thoughtfully*): Okay, here's being gay in a nutshell. I should reject you out of grief, thereby proving gay love is an authentic force for good. But the fact of the matter is every gay piece of meat is just a sketch for the next piece of meat, though you're just unbelievably cute, bitch. Did I already say that?

MACKEREL: I'm definitely it, dude. The buck stops here. Well, more specifically, here.

He gives his ass a playful slap.

MACKEREL: And, even more specifically, after heroin's in my system, if you're catching my drift.

Josh's boyfriend immediately pulls a big packet of nice looking dope out of his pocket.

JOSH'S BOYFRIEND: Deal. I love hicks.

MACKEREL: So I heard.

Josh's boyfriend holds out the packet, then seems to have a realization of some sort, and pulls it back.

JOSH'S BOYFRIEND: Wait, did you say Josh is dead? Let me guess, or did you already tell me?

MACKEREL (*impatiently*): Okay, fine. You know that guy Bin

Laden? I'm answering your question with a riddle. It's an old straight person trick from my childhood.

Josh's boyfriend: Sure, he's that famous person.

Mackerel: Okay, then what do you think of the trendy idea that all Americans died on 9/11? You know, that all of that shit with the planes proved we're all the same whatever in God's overall concept of whatever.

Josh's boyfriend: I'm into anything trendy. Just look around my living room. In fact, come on in. Where are my manners?

Mackerel: On one condition.

Josh's boyfriend: Deal. I mean what is it? Forgive the sleazy old chicken hawk in me. He'd go to prison for however many life terms to get it on with a thirteen-year-old ass, I mean your thirteen-year-old ass. That's a gay compliment. Enjoy.

Mackerel: The condition is that we travel to Pakistan together. On your credit cards, of course. There's a cute traitor guy over there I need to see. Long story. That's part one, and—this'll appeal to you—part two, I can get to Bin Laden. Check this out. So I overdose on heroin, right? I'm happy. Bin Laden rims my corpse. He's happy. You film it. Put the camera on a tripod, walk into the frame, and murder him with your bare fucking hands. Then turn off the camera and eat me. Everyone's happy, and gay guys rule the world. It's a no-brainer.

Josh's boyfriend: Are you psychic? I make snuff films for a living. Duh, right? That's how I paid for this gay upper-middle-class lifestyle you see before you. Wait, Josh told you I made snuff. Of course. You're not a psychic at all. I'm confused.

MACKEREL: Hunh. If I'd been gay a little longer, I'd say the real gay dilemma is that no amount of working out daily in a gym can make a guy your age interesting to someone my age. The mind goes. It's just a sad fact. I'm so not in the mood anymore. But yeah, I'm psychic.

JOSH'S BOYFRIEND: Then Pakistan it is. On one condition.

MACKEREL: It'd better involve dope.

JOSH'S BOYFRIEND: I'll pack my things, and—oh, it does—you strip and strike a nice doggie pose on my bed. I may be gay, but I'm not stupid. Well, not that stupid.

MACKEREL: Blahdiblahdiblah I mean deal.

An hour later, a very sore-assed Mackerel cracks the psychic's door and clears his throat. Josh's buff, elderly boyfriend is right behind him carrying their suitcases.

MACKEREL: Are you decent? I guess that's a relative term in your case.

PSYCHIC (*anxiously*): Who's there?

MACKEREL: God and a gay guy. Why, who's there?

PSYCHIC: Me, Allah's prying eyes, and some half-eaten teen whore. Wait, did you say God?

MACKEREL: And a gay guy, yeah. Coming in.

They enter the storefront. The psychic is sitting on the floor in front of Josh's dead body. He's holding a large, bloody knife, and Josh's once so perfect ass is no more, thanks to the psychic-turned-

cannibal's terrorist attacks. Josh's boyfriend leans over, looking around in the mini–ground zero.

JOSH'S BOYFRIEND: Josh? Is that your truth?
MACKEREL (*to the psychic*): That's a cue to do your thing.

The psychic shuts his eyes, and appears to go into a mystical trance.

PSYCHIC (*in a sixteen-year-old's voice*): What do you want, babe? I'm kind of busy. Being eaten is like getting fistfucked by the Colossus of Rhodes, only better.
JOSH'S BOYFRIEND: I told you.

He sets the suitcases down and reaches into the gore, then rips a chunk loose. He studies it carefully.

PSYCHIC (*in a sixteen-year-old's voice*): What do you want to know? I know everything there is to know now.
JOSH'S BOYFRIEND: How do you taste?
PSYCHIC (*in a sixteen-year-old's voice*): Like blood. That's too easy. You want to know how the world ends? You don't, trust me. It's so not sexy. It's so not gay.
JOSH'S BOYFRIEND: Does it have something to do with the gravitational pull of the dying sun?

He pops the chunk into his mouth and starts chewing.

PSYCHIC (*in a sixteen-year-old's voice*): Exactly. Boring.

JOSH'S BOYFRIEND: No offense, baby, but we saw that together on the Discovery Channel. By the way, yum.

MACKEREL: I have a question. Where's Bin Laden?

PSYCHIC (*in a sixteen-year-old's voice*): You! Hold on a second. First of all, seeing isn't knowing, babe. There's a huge metaphysical difference, it turns out. Now you, you little boyfriend-stealing white-trash bitch. You're supposed to be dead. I've been hanging out waiting for you. Cross your ass over here.

MACKEREL: Make me. No, seriously, where's Bin Laden? Don't make me unconjure you.

PSYCHIC (*in a sixteen-year-old's voice*): Kandahar. Satisfied?

MACKEREL: No.

PSYCHIC (*in a sixteen-year-old's voice*): Okay, ask my temporary form where Rakhid's Video is. Bin Laden's in the basement. Hey, you want to know how you die?

MACKEREL: As a hero. Unlike you.

PSYCHIC (*in a sixteen-year-old's voice*): Tsk tsk tsk. Tell him, babe.

JOSH'S BOYFRIEND: Tell him what, babe? Oh, right. You've been had. Chalk one up for us patient gay Capricorns.

MACKEREL: I'm not into astrology.

PSYCHIC (*in a sixteen-year-old's voice*): Fact, my boyfriend quote-unquote drives you to the airport. Fact, he makes a detour to pick something up at our house. Fact, the guys you stole that dope from are hiding inside. Fact, they rape and torture and whatever you for two days straight, then inject you with enough dope to kill Shaquille O'Neal, then rape your corpse for another two days. Right, babe?

JOSH'S BOYFRIEND: Pretty much. Well, rape in the broadest sense. If it's ever been called gay sex, it's in your future.

MACKEREL (*smugly*): A hero's still a hero. Arkansas boy's dream to save the world from Bin Laden crushed by evil pedophile ring. Americans love that shit.

PSYCHIC (*in a sixteen-year-old's voice*): Yeah, until they do the autopsy and find enough sperm in your ass to start a small third world country. We'll see how heroic you are after they drag your whorish, drugged-out lifestyle through the tabloids.

MACKEREL: Well, at least I have an ass. At least my ass isn't digested. At least my ass isn't some low-end Al Qaeda water boy's Taco fucking Bell. Say something, gay guy. Defend me. What kind of sugar daddy are you?

Josh's boyfriend stops ripping out pieces of the ass and popping them into his mouth.

JOSH'S BOYFRIEND: Look, Josh. Realism, okay? I'm gay, you're dead, he's thirteen years old, you saw his ass, what do you expect? Is death like Alzheimer's or something?

PSYCHIC (*in a sixteen-year-old's voice*): Forget it. So how do I taste anyway? Honestly.

JOSH'S BOYFRIEND: Like blood. Not that I'm complaining.

Mackerel was resigned to his fate as the world's most extremely murdered boy until they reached Josh's boyfriend's front door.

Now he's taken a nervous step backward, and his face is clouded over with thinking.

JOSH'S BOYFRIEND: What now? Your death has so much baggage.

MACKEREL (*ominously*): I feel them. I don't mean psychically. I mean whatchacallit, that humanistic word.

JOSH'S BOYFRIEND: Go somewhere more specific with "them" first. I'm no humanist. And when you're gay, "them" just means straight. So define "them," and quickly.

He looks at his watch.

MACKEREL: The former me's. Cute boys.

JOSH'S BOYFRIEND: You mean like old what's-his-name, my ex?

MACKEREL: For instance.

JOSH'S BOYFRIEND: So you feel like a blip? Like it's cool I'm so cute to one older rich gay guy and all, but it's not like he's Barry Diller? 'Cos that was old what's-his-name's beef, if memory serves.

MACKEREL: Empathically. That's the word I was looking for.

JOSH'S BOYFRIEND: Break it down.

MACKEREL: Love without sex.

JOSH'S BOYFRIEND: Whoa. Just hold on a minute. What the hell are you saying? This is so early Edmund White. You're far too young to remember him. He wrote novels. Do you know what novels are?

MACKEREL: Was Edmund White like Proust? Please say yes.

JOSH'S BOYFRIEND: Yes. Not that I've read Proust. Like all gay guys, I haven't read a novel since 1994.

MACKEREL: I'm too good for you. What does it mean?

JOSH'S BOYFRIEND: It means you're the ultimate twink. That's why we all keep rimming you. You're God. Enjoy.

MACKEREL: But you don't fistfuck God.

JOSH'S BOYFRIEND: Says who?

MACKEREL: The Bible.

JOSH'S BOYFRIEND: You don't have a Bible yet. You have to die first. I promise you it'll be Proustian, whatever that means. I'll buy a thesaurus, whatever that is. I'll put in lots and lots of sex so gay guys will buy it. I'll make you look like whomever you want. Name it.

MACKEREL: Okay, who's the cutest boy in the world?

JOSH'S BOYFRIEND: You got it.

He raises his voice such that the tweaking, soon-to-be gay murderers inside his house will hear every word distinctly.

JOSH'S BOYFRIEND: Guys, cutest boy in the world. What's your guess?

Thousands of muffled, gay-sounding voices yell names enthusiastically at the same exact moment.

JOSH'S BOYFRIEND: One at a time. On second thought, pick a leader.

MACKEREL: They don't deserve me. This is super depressing.

MUFFLED GAY-SOUNDING VOICE: Okay, we've got your results. But they're too close to call. How about we just narrow it down, and give you a choice? Any of them will do. You can't lose.

MACKEREL: Agreed. By the way, who are you, leader guy, so I'll know who's the top?

MUFFLED GAY-SOUNDING VOICE: Me? Carl's my name. I'll tell you what. Here's who I used to be, because I'm just a forty-ish, ugly, gay, gym-going dreg who watches too much porn now. But I used to be the slightly queeny but cute enough to make up for it blond boy who hung around in West Hollywood back in the '80s, if you remember that?

JOSH'S BOYFRIEND: He's thirteen, dope. But I remember you. It's me, Lawrence, the old but muscular enough to make up for it guy. Ring a bell?

MUFFLED GAY-SOUNDING VOICE: Ding, yeah. How's it hanging?

JOSH'S BOYFRIEND: It's hanging, dude.

MUFFLED GAY-SOUNDING VOICE: God bless the past, right?

JOSH'S BOYFRIEND: You said it.

MUFFLED GAY-SOUNDING VOICE: Anyway, according to our poll, the cutest boys in the world are Taylor Hanson circa "MMMBop," duh. Aaron Carter at any age, under any circumstances, duh. Devon Sawa circa that TV movie called something like *Tornado*. Aaron Carter. Nick Carter before he got chunky. Leonardo DiCaprio pre–*The Beach*. And did I say Aaron Carter? If not, Aaron Carter.

JOSH'S BOYFRIEND: Tough choice.

Mackerel: Who's the first one he said again?

Josh's boyfriend: Taylor Hanson circa "MMMBop."

Mackerel: Him.

Josh's boyfriend (*yelling*): He chose early Taylor Hanson. How hot is that?

Muffled gay-sounding voice: Shit. Fine, we're so horny and fucked up on crystal meth that we'll deal with the fact that he isn't Aaron Carter.

Josh's boyfriend (*to Mackerel, whispering*): Pick Aaron Carter.

Mackerel: Why?

Josh's boyfriend: Why?! Am I losing my mind?

Mackerel: You mean that "Aaron's Party" dork?

Josh's boyfriend: Bingo.

Mackerel (*mournfully*): Him then. But your pettiness is giving me pause.

Behind Josh's boyfriend's front door, the muffled good news spreads and muffled zippers start unzipping.

Josh's boyfriend: So any last words? I mean before you just start saying ouch and all that?

Mackerel: Yeah, actually. Let history record that a boy who only wanted to serve humanity by serving himself was sidetracked by the jihad that homoeroticism has unleashed upon the cute. My intellect could have saved us, had we known me, but my ass was too great a distraction, albeit for quite understandable reasons. That's it, I guess. Oh, and a secret. I was just a straight boy who liked being rimmed and told older gay guys he was gay because his girlfriends were so prissy. I don't deserve to die gay, therefore. Think about it. After you've thought about it, talk to me through a psychic of your choice, and I'll tell you the truth of life. Then blow yourselves up in a crowded place. See if I care. Oh, and anarchy rules.

JOSH'S BOYFRIEND: You have a point. But you're so fucking cute.

MACKEREL (*sourly*): Let's just do it, okay?

He puts his hand on the doorknob.

MACKEREL: But thanks. I am, aren't I? Tell the world.

About the author

About the book

Read on

Insights,
Interviews
& More . . .

A Conversation with Dennis Cooper

Yuri Smirnov

Robert Glück interviewed Dennis Cooper for Narrativity, *issue 3.*

Robert Glück: *I have a theory that we pretty much become the writers we wanted to be in the first place. When you first began to write, what was your idea of the writing life, yourself in it? Who were your models? What were the attractions? How did you see yourself in twenty or thirty years? Did your writing itself take you in a different direction from that, or are you now pretty much what you imagined you would be?*

Dennis Cooper: Well, my idea of the writing life was very impractical and romantic. But then I was fifteen, so I guess that makes sense. My first model was—and, in a weird way, still is—Rimbaud. Finding his work is what made me decide to devote my life to writing. At that point in my life, I was extremely interested in the effects of psychedelic drugs and related rock music, and I think Rimbaud's notion that language could be fashioned into a spell that summoned ulterior or poetic knowledge represented a practical way to pursue this interest. My other model at that point was Sade, but in that case it was a matter of his work waking me up to my own preexisting fascinations and legitimizing them as a subject for writing. As a person, he didn't appeal to me at all. My third important model was and is Robert Bresson, but I didn't find his work until I was in my early twenties. His films made my work start to fall into place.

I think the attraction of writing was its secrecy, and that I could do it with absolute independence and in complete privacy. My personal life was both externally and internally very chaotic at that point, so these qualities really appealed to me. I didn't have to think about whether what I was thinking and writing was insane or sick because no one knew what I was doing. In fact, I didn't show my "real" work to anyone for many years. Even when I was first publishing my poetry, I never considered that to be my real work. The poetry and my early prose poems were ways for me develop my chops and test the waters. In secret, I was developing what ended up being my cycle of novels. I don't know that I could have worked that way in any form other than writing.

I must have imagined who I would ▸

“I think the attraction of writing was its secrecy, and that I could do it with absolute independence and in complete privacy.”

A Conversation with Dennis Cooper
(continued)

be in twenty or thirty years, but I don't really remember. It's a pretty safe guess to say that I saw myself being like Rimbaud, Sade, and Bresson, which I suppose means an artist who was known and respected, and whose work was very important to some people but not necessarily known to or loved by all.

Well, I guess I did become the writer I imagined I'd be, didn't I? My work seems to mean a lot to a certain kind of young person, and I get a lot of really moving e-mails and letters from young writers who say my work inspired them to write. So I guess your theory makes sense. Of course I never imagined the whole publishing world nonsense and the difficulty of cracking the literary establishment and the lack of financial reward for being this kind of writer. But, yeah, when I'm discouraged by the insurmountable problems that my work creates for itself and for me, realizing that I've achieved what I dreamed of achieving keeps me on track. So, Bob, can I assume that you became the writer you imagined, too? I'd really like to know, if you don't mind making this interview somewhat of a conversation.

“But, yeah, when I'm discouraged by the insurmountable problems that my work creates for itself and for me, realizing that I've achieved what I dreamed of achieving keeps me on track.”

RG: *Well, okay, briefly. Though I never believed in God, I wanted to be a saint and for divinity to pour through me, so I may have missed the mark. I lived in almost total isolation; I wanted contact and a kind of absolute. It made me ambitious* *for literature itself and suspicious of personal ambition. I think Rimbaud is the summit of that kind of writer. He opposes his culture, expresses its instability, and he wants words to actually move mountains, start revolutions. But my very first love was for John Keats, a surface smooth as enamel, and underneath a heart breaking against an absolute. There is some way he wills things into words, almost three-dimensionally, like the drops of blood on a Flemish crucifixion. If I had known the term, I would have said cult writer, recognized by few. I imagined my perfect reader to be someone digging through a bin of used books, attracted by a deeply strange volume which alters his life in some way. . . .*

DC: That's beautiful, and pretty close to my dreams. I wonder if Keats is the distinguishing factor.

RG: *Rimbaud certainly was a poet to lead you into the present. I love your poems—don't disparage them! I am curious if there are some passages from Rimbaud that are still in your head, and what you think about them. And I'd really like to know more about the inner and outer chaos you mention. You often talk about Bresson. Could you tell me a particular film that was important, and go into it a ways?*

DC: Rimbaud is a writer I've reread at least once a year, so I don't really have a sterling, isolated memory of the ▸

A Conversation with Dennis Cooper
(continued)

particulars that first hooked me on him. I know it was a combination of *A Season in Hell* and his letters—the external and the internal, as it were. My fondness is generalized, and has to do with the superior translations of his work, especially Enid Peschel's versions of *A Season in Hell* and "The Drunken Boat." I think it's sad and vaguely criminal that most widely available translations of Rimbaud in English are Paul Schmidt's, because his *Illuminations* and *Season in Hell* don't begin to cut it.

Fifteen was a really important age for me. I decided to become a writer. I met George Miles, who would become my muse and the most important and influential person I would know in my life. I started using drugs as an investigative tool. I had sex for the first time and realized I was gay. I found a group of similarly artsy, intelligent friends and was suddenly cool. All these things helped me start to get away from a life that had been very confusing and unstable. Before then I was a profoundly unpopular kid who was harassed and beaten up at school, and spent most of my time in my bedroom obsessing over rock music and television shows, drawing pictures and writing naive poems and stories. Not to mention that I was tormented by the thrills I'd felt when three boys my age were found raped and murdered in the mountains near my house two years before. My parents were in the middle

"Fifteen was a really important age for me. I decided to become a writer. I met George Miles, who would become my muse . . . I started using drugs as an investigative tool."

of really ugly and protracted divorce proceedings. My mother, whom I lived with, began drinking very heavily and her behavior was unpredictable and very chaotic throughout my early teens. I'm the oldest of four kids, which made me feel responsible for my siblings, whom I couldn't protect. It was all really terrifying, so having that revelation at fifteen about who I was made a huge difference. It helped me separate myself from all that to some extent. I could escape into writing or drugs. I could crash at my friends' houses whenever I wanted. I could focus my thwarted wish to cure my mom or protect my siblings on George, who was deeply troubled, but, at the same time, someone not unlike myself, and who seemed to really flourish within my love and support for a long time.

My favorite Bresson film is *The Devil, Probably (Le Diable Probablement)*, mainly because its concerns are so close to my own. The first Bresson film I saw, and the one that changed my life, was *Lancelot du Lac.* It's an astonishing work, though I think if I'd seen any of his other films first, it would have had the same effect. His work is so powerful and meaningful to me that I find it almost impossible to talk about. It's like his influence dawned on me rather than being something I studied into being. It's something to do with his work's concision in relationship to the ephemeral and chaotic nature of his ▸

A Conversation with Dennis Cooper
(continued)

subject matter. And that it's nothing but style and form on the one hand, and completely transparent and pure on the other. It's only concerned with emotional truth, and, at the same time, it works so hard to exclude all superficial signs of emotion. It's bleakness incarnate and yet it's almost obsessively sympathetic to the deepest human feelings in a way that can only read as hopeful. It's religious art and, yet, despite Bresson's avowed Catholicism, it seems not to depend on any religious system for answers or comfort. The fact that Bresson only used non-actors inspired me to create characters in my work who were non-characters in a sense—that is characters who seem both unworthy of the attentions of art and incapable of collaborating with art in the traditional sense. That relationship between Bresson and his "actors" was very key to me, and if you read his book *Notes on Cinematography*, it's all there. I could go on and on, but that's a general explanation, I guess.

To read the full interview visit http://www.sfsu.edu/~poetry/narrativity/issue_three/gluck.html

Vast Inspiration
The Cooper Lists

My Fifty Favorite Poems (In No Order)

(1) Arthur Rimbaud, *A Season in Hell*, (2) James Schuyler, "This Dark Apartment," (3) John Ashbery, "A Wave," (4) Kenward Elmslie, "Girl Machine," (5) Judy Grahn, "A Woman Is Talking to Death," (6) Joe Brainard, "I Remember," (7) Ted Berrigan, *The Sonnets*, (8) Frank O'Hara, "For the Chinese New Year & for Bill Berkson," (9) Alice Notley, "How Spring Comes," (10) John Wieners, "Act #2," (11) Lyn Hejinian, *My Life*, (12) Eileen Myles, "Promotional Material," (13) Ron Koertge, "Coming Out," (14) Ron Padgett, "After the Broken Arm," (15) Amy Gerstler, "The Fetus' Curious Monologue," (16) James Tate, "Absences," (17) Bill Knott, "Death," (18) Jerome Sala, "The New Sadness," (19) Elaine Equi, "Voice-Over," (20) Tim Dlugos, "G-9," (21) Donald Britton, "Santa," (22) Bob Flanagan, *Slave Sonnets*, (23) Bernard Welt, "I stopped writing poetry . . . ," (24) Ed Smith, "Untitled (Tonight I aspire . . .)," (25) Jack Skelley, "Whammo Amnesia," (26) Ai, "The Kid," (27) James Wright, "Lying in a Hammock at William Duffy's Farm in Pine Island, Minnesota," (28) David Trinidad, "Of Mere Plastic," (29) Bernadette Mayer, *Studying Hunger*, (30) Ron Silliman, *Tjanting*, (31) Kevin Killian, "Four Flies on Gray Velvet," (32) Michael Lassell, "How to Watch

Vast Inspiration ***(continued)***

Your Brother Die," (33) Jack Spicer, *Billy the Kid*, (34) Kenneth Koch, "The Circus," (35) Tom Clark, "Neil Young," (36) Sylvia Plath, "Daddy," (37) Sappho, "To One Who Loves Not Poetry," (38) Constantin Cavafy, "He Came to Read," (39) Charles Baudelaire, "The Remorse of the Dead," (40) Antonin Artaud, "Artaud le Momo," (41) Olivier Cadiot, "The Shipwreck," (42) Clark Coolidge, *Mine: The One That Enters the Stories*, (43) Brad Gooch, "A dome of shiny met," (44) James Krusoe, "Two Poems with My Father in Them," (45) Peter Schjeldahl, "I Missed Punk," (46) Rene Ricard, "The Slaves of Michelangelo," (47) Robert Glück, "Invaders from Mars," (48) Pierre Reverdy, "Miracle," (49) René Char, "Forehead of the Rose," (50) Paul Celan, "Epitaph for François."

My Fifty Favorite Novels (In No Order)

(1) The Marquis de Sade, *The 120 Days of Sodom*, (2) Maurice Blanchot, *Death Sentence*, (3) Jean Genet, *Funeral Rites*, (4) Jean Rhys, *Good Morning, Midnight*, (5) Thomas Bernhard, *Wittgenstein's Nephew*, (6) J. D. Salinger, *The Catcher in the Rye*, (7) Max Frisch, *Man in the Holocene*, (8) Agota Kristof, *The Notebook/The Proof/The Third Lie*, (9) Kathy Acker, *Great Expectations*, (10) Thomas Mann, *Death in Venice*, (11) Gustave Flaubert, *A Sentimental Education*, (12) J. G. Ballard, *The Atrocity Exhibition*, (13) Robert Pinget, *Fable*, (14) Alain Robbe-Grillet, *Recollection of*

the Golden Triangle, (15) Claude Simon, *Triptych*, (16) Nathalie Sarraute, *The Golden Fruits*, (17) William S. Burroughs, *The Wild Boys*, (18) André Gide, *The Counterfeiters*, (19) Georges Bataille, *Story of the Eye*, (20) Thomas Pynchon, *Mason & Dixon*, (21) David Foster Wallace, *Infinite Jest*, (22) Bret Easton Ellis, *American Psycho*, (23) James McCourt, *Time Remaining*, (24) Ivy Compton-Burnett, *The Present and the Past*, (25) Comte de Lautréamont, *Maldoror*, (26) Ishmael Reed, *The Freelance Pallbearers*, (27) Hervé Guibert, *The Compassion Protocol*, (28) S. E. Hinton, *The Outsiders*, (29) Louis-Ferdinand Céline, *Death on the Installment Plan*, (30) Raymond Roussel, *Locus Solus*, (31) Pierre Guyotat, *Eden Eden Eden*, (32) Philippe Sollers, *Event*, (33) Ronald Firbank, *The Flower Beneath the Foot*, (34) Georges Perec, *Life: A User's Manual*, (35) William Gaddis, *Carpenter's Gothic*, (36) Sadegh Hedayat, *The Blind Owl*, (37) Robert Glück, *Jack the Modernist*, (38) Kevin Killian, *Shy*, (39) Dodie Bellamy, *The Letters of Mina Harker*, (40) Robert Walser, *Jakob von Gunten*, (41) Denton Welch, *In Youth Is Pleasure*, (42) Italo Calvino, *If on a Winter's Night a Traveler*, (43) Joan Didion, *Play It as It Lays*, (44) Raymond Queneau, *Exercises in Style*, (45) Yasunari Kawabata, *Snow Country*, (46) Steven Millhauser, *Edwin Mullhouse*, (47) Tony Duvert, *Strange Landscape*, (48) Cormac McCarthy, *Child of God*, (49) Philip K.

Vast Inspiration ***(continued)***

Dick, *Ubik*, (50) Pierre Klossowski, *Roberte Ce Soir*.

My Fifty Favorite Robert Pollard and/or Guided by Voices Songs (In No Order)

(1) Guided by Voices, "Redmen and Their Wives," *Under the Bushes Under the Stars*; (2) Robert Pollard, "Far-out Crops," *Kid Marine*; (3) GBV, "14 Cheerleader Coldfront," *Propeller*; (4) GBV, "Little Whirl," *Alien Lanes*; (5) GBV, "My Impression Now," *Fast Japanese Spin Cycle*; (6) GBV, "The Best of Jill Hives," *Earthquake Glue*; (7) RP, "And My Unit Moves," *Speak Kindly of Your Volunteer Fire Department*; (8) GBV, "Dayton, Ohio—19 Something and 5," *Tonics and Twisted Chasers*; (9) GBV, "Liquid Indian," *Do the Collapse*; (10) RP, "White Gloves Come Off," *KM*; (11) RP, "The Ash Gray Proclamation," *Not in My Airforce*; (12) GBV, "A Salty Salute," *AL*; (13) GBV, "Awful Bliss," *Bee Thousand*; (14) RP, "I Get Rid of You," *SKOYVFD*; (15) GBV, "Johnny Appleseed," *Clown Prince of the Menthol Trailer*; (16) RP, "Kickboxer Lightning," *Choreographed Man of War*; (17) GBV, "Chicken Blows," *AL*; (18) GBV, "Exit Flagger," *Propeller*; (19) GBV, "Kicker of Elves," *BT*; (20) GBV, "Don't Stop Now," *UTBUTS*; (21) GBV, "Father Sgt. Christmas Card," *Universal Truths and Cycles*; (22) GBV, "Tractor Rape Chain," *BT*; (23) GBV, "Huffman Prairie Flying Field," *Half Smiles of the Decomposed*; (24) GBV, "Run Wild," *Isolation Drills*; (25) RP, "Pop Zeus," *SKOYVFD*; (26) Airport 5,

"The Cost of Shipping Cattle," *Tower in the Fountain of Sparks*; (27) RP, "Vibrations in the Woods," *Waved Out*; (28) RP, "Trial of Affliction and Light Sleeping," *Fiction Man*; (29) RP, "40 Yards to the Burning Bush," *CMOW*; (30) GBV, "Game of Pricks," *AL*; (31) A5, "Stifled Man Casino," *TITFOS*; (32) A5, "How Brown?" *Life Starts Here*; (33) GBV, "Melted Pat," *Get out of My Stations*; (34) GBV, "Do the Earth," *I Am a Scientist*; (35) GBV, "Cut-out Witch," *UTBUTS*; (36) GBV, "Queen of Cans and Jars," *BT*; (37) GBV, "Back to the Lake," *UTAC*; (38) GBV, "Lethargy," *Propeller*; (39) GBV, "Motor Away," *AL*; (40) GBV, "The Official Ironman Rally Song," *UTBUTS*; (41) RP, "Love Is Stronger than Witchcraft," *From a Compound Eye*; (42) RP, "Subspace Biographies," *WO*; (43) GBV, "Car Language," *UTAC*; (44) GBV, "The Goldheart Mountaintop Queen Directory," *BT*; (45) GBV, "Wrecking Now," *DTC*; (46) GBV, "Little Lines," *Mag Earwhig!*; (47) GBV, "How's My Drinking?" *ID*; (48) GBV, "Atom Eyes," *UTBUTS*; (49) GBV, "Non-absorbing," *VOT*; (50) RP, "Town of Mirrors," *KM*.

My Fifty Favorite Songs (In No Order)

(1) Sebadoh, "Brand New Love," (2) Captain Beefheart and the Magic Band, "Big Eyed Beans from Venus," (3) ABBA, "Knowing Me, Knowing You," (4) Spirit, "Aren't You Glad," (5) Robert Pollard, "White Gloves Come Off," (6) Serge Lama, "Je Suis Malade,"

Vast Inspiration ***(continued)***

(7) Brecht/Weill, "Song of the Insufficiency of Human Endeavor," (8) The Dickies, "Fan Mail," (9) Leonard Cohen, "Famous Blue Raincoat," (10) Xiu Xiu, "Blacks," (11) The Velvet Underground, "White Light/White Heat," (12) The Quick, "Teacher's Pet," (13) Jesus and Mary Chain, "The Hardest Walk," (14) Wire, "From the Nursery," (15) Björk, "Hyper-ballad," (16) Alexander O'Neal, "Criticize," (17) The Ramones, "I Don't Wanna Go Down to the Basement," (18) Pink Floyd, "Lucifer Sam," (19) Neil Young, "Tired Eyes," (20) Donovan, "Epistle to Dippy," (21) Pavement, "Grounded," (22) Magazine, "The Light Pours out of Me," (23) Superchunk, "Untied," (24) Television, "See No Evil," (25) Public Enemy, "Bring the Noise," (26) Beach Boys, "Cabinessence," (27) Sonic Youth, "Schizophrenia," (28) The New Pornographers, "Use It," (29) The Sex Pistols, "Anarchy in the U.K.," (30) Soft Cell, "Say Hello, Wave Goodbye," (31) Guided by Voices, "Redmen and Their Wives," (32) The Flaming Lips, "The Spiderbite Song," (33) Jefferson Airplane, "Watch Her Ride," (34) Slayer, "Raining Blood," (35) Hüsker Dü, "Pink Turns to Blue," (36) Sparks, "Mickey Mouse," (37) Eno, "The True Wheel," (38) My Bloody Valentine, "Cigarettes in Your Bed," (39) Steely Dan, "Charlie Freak," (40) Spacemen 3, "O.D.Catastrophe," (41) Randy Newman, "The World Isn't Fair," (42) Peter Green's Fleetwood Mac,

"The Green Manalishi (with the Two-Pronged Crown)," (43) The Shangri-Las, "Past, Present, and Future," (44) XTC, "Rocket from a Bottle," (45) Tim Buckley, "Pleasant Street," (46) David Ackles, "Montana Song," (47) The Fall, "Cruiser's Creek," (48) Cheap Trick, "Auf Wiedersehen," (49) Gram Parsons, "$1000 Wedding," (50) Rolling Stones, "We Love You."

My Fifty Favorite Films (In No Order)

(1) Robert Bresson, *The Devil, Probably*, (2) Robert Bresson, *Lancelot du Lac*, (3) Robert Bresson, *Four Nights of a Dreamer*, (4) Andy Warhol, *Chelsea Girls*, (5) Orson Welles, *The Magnificent Ambersons*, (6) Alain Resnais, *Providence*, (7) Sergei Paradjanov, *The Color of Pomegranates*, (8) Yasujiro Ozu, *Late Spring*, (9) Kenneth Anger, *The Inauguration of the Pleasure Dome*, (10) James Benning, *11 x 17*, (11) Bernardo Bertolucci, *Luna*, (12) Rainer Werner Fassbinder, *In a Year of 13 Moons*, (13) Werner Herzog, *Stroszek*, (14) Wes Anderson, *Rushmore*, (15) John Huston, *The Dead*, (16) Jean-Luc Godard, *Pierrot le Fou*, (17) Hollis Frampton, *Magellan Cycle*, (18) Luchino Visconti, *Death in Venice*, (19) Chris Marker, *Le Jetée*, (20) Tim Hunter, *River's Edge*, (21) David Lynch, *Lost Highway*, (22) Gaspar Noé, *Irreversible*, (23) Jean-Daniel Cadinot, *All of Me*, (24) Walt Disney, *Pinocchio*, (25) Stanley Kubrick, *Dr. Strangelove*, (26) Andy Warhol, *Lonesome Cowboys*, (27) Maya

Vast Inspiration: ***(continued)***

Deren, *Ritual in Transfigured Time*, (28) Stan Brakhage, *Dog Star Man*, (29) Ingmar Bergman, *Hour of the Wolf*, (30) Luis Buñuel, *The Exterminating Angel*, (31) Robert Altman, *McCabe & Mrs. Miller*, (32) Terrence Malick, *The Thin Red Line*, (33) Terrence Malick, *Days of Heaven*, (34) Federico Fellini, *Satyricon*, (35) Jacques Rivette, *Céline and Julie Go Boating*, (36) Michelangelo Antonioni, *Blow-Up*, (37) Errol Morris, *Fast, Cheap & Out of Control*, (38) The Coen Brothers, *Fargo*, (39) Robert Bresson, *L'Argent*, (40) Robert Bresson, *Pickpocket*, (41) Alexander Kluges, *Artists Under the Big Top: Disoriented*, (42) Jacques Tati, *Play Time*, (43) Eric Rohmer, *Perceval le Gallois*, (44) Tobe Hooper, *The Texas Chainsaw Massacre*, (45) Terrence Malick, *The New World*, (46) David Cronenberg, *Videodrome*, (47) Stanley Kubrick, *A Clockwork Orange*, (48) Straub-Huillet, *Chronicle of Anna Magdalena Bach*, (49) Ryan Trecartin, *A Family Finds Entertainment*, (50) John Waters, *Serial Mom*.

Five Poems

The Faint

for Paul Otchakovsky-Laurens

This is an immaterial poem about a ghost,
name of Dennis. I appear less important
to those few among you who knew me
when I was composed more realistically.

Once my empty sockets seemed like evil
eyes to you, and you had no idea their
trick wasn't great art. Now I barely exist,
but train your sights on this nevertheless.

It's past your bedtime. I've painted myself
into a corner. A ghost has been sketched
here haphazardly. I'm still myself but
    inspire
no illusions no matter how I'm executed.

To believe in a ghost was small potatoes
next to the fear in your eyes. I scared you.
All I was is this marked up white sheet, so
I ask you again. Read into my black holes.

November 17, 1987

George goes to bed depressed.
He wakes up suicidal and more.
Something has really changed.
If he had a gun, he'd know what.

If he lived somewhere else he
might drag his ass onto some
bridge over whatever river and
feel too scared to throw it off.

What happened last night, day,
or before that on the weekend?
Wished he had a gun, but way
before that in total innocence?

He'd slip one finger in the trigger.
Who'd know? Put the barrel to
his head. Who'd say why not?
No one else, but he would pull it.

The Green Album

"Great!" she yelled
when I reached inside her
to the elbow
and my hand tried
a slow dance with a lung,

when her back ripped
and sprayed us
under the lightning of my belt
as she crawled into
the quicksand of my bed,

when I choked her woozy,
raised the toilet lid
and punched her face
until she saw the necklace
I'd given her.

You know who
you fucked. If
she's my wife,
so what. Soon
you will be me.
If it's her, you
so screwed. If
not, she lies to
you, on top of
everyone else.
I'll tell you this.
You're fucking
evil, if you did.

Five Poems ***(continued)***

She's so dead. If I want
her ass again, I need to
love it. If I don't want it
enough to scare myself,

then I don't. I broke her
jaw. Yeah, I see that.
Can't you comprehend?
Yeah, I'll think about it.

There's a guy who's just
shit from his dad when
he's expected to fuck what
he loves and I'm that shit.

E.H.

Not to brag but if one more muffled voice jokes, "Your ass could teach a poetry workshop," or "I don't know what's cooking in that oven, but can I invite myself for dinner?" or "Don't mind me, I'm just looking for the cure for colon cancer," or "I'm no Freud, but I can tell you why the guy who cleaned the bathrooms at your kindergarten paid you $20 not to flush," or "If I suffocate, tell my mom I loved her," or "Just call me Jules Verne," or "You should list your anal membranes on the stock market," or "I never thought I'd say this, but I envy Gene Simmons," or "Fuck man, what did you eat for dinner, God?" or "Next time I'm in a bar, I'm going to order your douche," I'm going to scream.

The jpegs

39 yr old poz Black stud wants to seed
a neg ass. I'm a recent ex-con, straight,
Bernie Mac–type who got pozzed sharing
needles in prison. I like the idea of killing
guys this way. Plus it don't violate my
parole.

Listen, Bernie. This death sentence
rhetoric is from twenty years ago. You
can bareback for years before anything
really bad happens. Take your depressing
shit elsewhere. I'm a neg bottom and Ray
Romano look-alike hoping to be bred by
hung poz (status and outlook) tops.

Ray, Bernie here. I like your attitude. Can
I kill you?

"The Faint," "November 17, 1987," "The Green Album," "E.H.," and "The jpegs" were previously published in the limited edition book, The Weaklings, *in 2008 by Fanzine Press, and are reprinted by permission of the author.*